WE
ALL
SLEEP
IN
THE
SAME
ROOM

THIS IS A GENUINE BARNACLE BOOK

A Barnacle Book | Rare Bird Books
453 South Spring Street, Suite 531
Los Angeles, CA 90013
abarnaclebook.com
rarebirdbooks.com

Set in Goudy Old Style
Printed in the United States of America
Distributed in the U.S. by Publishers Group West

10 9 8 7 6 5 4 3 2 1

Publisher's Cataloging-in-Publication data

Rome, Paul.
    We all sleep in the same room : a novel / by Paul Rome.
    p. cm.
    ISBN 9780985490294

1. Law firms—Fiction. 2. Manhattan (New York, N.Y.)—Fiction.
3. Brooklyn (New York, N.Y.)—Fiction. 4. Family—Fiction. I. Title.

PS3618.O596 W4 2013
813.6 —dc23

for my father

When the smoky clouds hung low in the west and the red sun went down behind them, leaving a pink flush on the snowy roofs and the blue drifts, then the wind sprang up afresh with a kind of bitter song, as if it said: "This is reality, whether you like it or not. All those frivolities of summer, the light and shadow, the living mask of green that trembled over everything, they were lies, and this is what was underneath."

—Willa Cather, My Ántonia

September

1

When I first see them together, it's from a distance, between passing cars: Frank Gordon carrying my son, Ben, down Park Avenue South. Then they're at the corner where 17th Street meets Union Square, pausing for the light to change. Ben's arms are wrapped around Frank's neck so that Frank's face is obscured. The two of them appear to be bobbing gently up and down.

When they reach the other corner, Ben is carefully lowered to the ground, and I see for the first time Frank's face. He's Asian. Raina hadn't mentioned that.

According to Frank's resume, he graduated in May with a BFA in graphic design from SVA.

This is a selling point for Raina. In another lifetime, Raina might have happily skipped communications and gone for art school, to devote herself fully to photography. This other Raina, the up-and-coming photographer, probably never would have stopped in 1984 to strike up conversation with the clean-cut young man handing out flyers to protest the lousy living conditions maintained by a few sleazy East Village slumlords. That was me, once.

Frank whispers something in Ben's ear. Then the two of them are running in my direction—Ben wobbling as fast as he can. Ben runs right past me, where I've been leaning against an adjacent stairwell, and slaps his palms against the front door of our building.

"You beat me," Frank calls. He's stopped running and now saunters forward. Our eyes converge. He seems to give me an elongated once-over.

I was the one who selected Frank's reply from the dozens of others we received in response to our Craigslist post. We were scrambling. Raina had gradually, in the first June heat wave, and then decisively, as the humidity crescendoed in mid-August, made up her mind to rejoin the workforce. And with characteristic lack of hesitancy, she'd soon thereafter committed to a managerial role, a return to her very first career as art director for a lifestyle magazine. Amid Raina's drafting of cover letters, Bernadette, our reticent but trusted nanny, had given two weeks' notice with kind words and the enigmatic vagueness befitting the personality she'd allowed us to know during the year of her employment. Raina and I both agreed Ben was ready for a babysitter. Someone who could, and would, engage him rather than just change his diapers. A young man would be ideal. I was attracted to Frank's direct prose and his unadorned enthusiasm for afternoons spent in the park. You could trust a young guy with a sharp résumé and a name like Frank Gordon.

I swoop in behind Ben and throw him up high above my head, spin him around, and lower him to my face.

"Daddy," he says.

I turn with son in arms and extend a hand to Frank.

"Hello," I say. "I'm Tom, Ben's father."

"Daddy, I want to get down."

"Frank," says Frank. "It's nice to meet you. I was wondering who was watching us."

At half-a-head shorter, Frank is required to peer up at me. Brushing away locks of his surprisingly long hair, he offers a youthful smile. I unlock the door and welcome everyone inside.

Ben leads the way, attacking the stairs like a cub, using his short arms as front legs to propel himself forward. Frank follows with a wide grin, undoubtedly amused by the act of a three-year-old climbing stairs.

Raina is waiting at the landing.

"Mommy!" cries Ben, forgoing his lion-like leaps for his fastest sprint to her arms, where, nose-to-nose, they share a collective burst of joyous, incomprehensible baby talk.

"You're home early," I say. "I thought you had a staff meeting."

Raina's beaming, unexpected presence makes superfluous my earlier efforts in re-scheduling a partners meeting and a conference call with reps from the American Federation of Teachers. We'd discussed all of it the night before. But I know better than to say something which might affect Frank's initial impression of my wife's and my decision-making as anything other than unified.

"Yeah, there was a meeting," she says, "but I got too impatient. I wanted to see my big guy."

She unleashes another succession of kisses upon Ben's face. Then she turns to Frank, who stands next to me in the stairwell. "How was your first day together?"

"A lot of fun," Frank says. "We rode the subway to the park, and Ben made friends with a girl named Ella. Then he walked home five of the blocks on his own, and I carried him the rest of the way."

Ben spreads his arms into the air while still held against Raina. The conversation has already bypassed him and his mind is elsewhere. He's mimicking a plane or Dumbo sailing through the circus tent.

"That's good," I say. "That's good he made it that far."

Last Tuesday, when I got caught up working late at the office with Jessie, I phoned Raina to say she ought to go ahead and conduct the interview with Frank without me. Her account over coffee the next morning was curious. She flushed. Then she reported that they had spoken for maybe ten minutes, maybe less, and when he got up to go she'd blurted out, *I can tell you're the one.* She agreed it was a bit impulsive, but she'd felt absolutely certain about him from the second he walked in, and didn't want him to accept an offer elsewhere. Ben seemed to really like him too, she told me. She said he radiated a certain honesty and warmth.

"So Ben didn't work you too hard? I mean, you're going to stay with us?" Raina says.

"So far, so good." Frank says.

"Wonderful, I'm so pleased," Raina says. "It's great that Ben has a new afternoon companion. Now say goodbye to Frank," my wife instructs our son. "Tell him, *thanks Frank, I had a nice day.*"

Ben snaps out of his dream world and whispers into Raina's ear.

"You tell him," Raina says, but to Ben's vigorously shaking head, she yields: "Okay, okay, alright, I'll ask him. Frank, would you like to come in and see Ben's trains?"

* * *

I RETURN HOME WITH a fresh set of keys. Ben's new companion is crawling on the carpet, pulling a train along a newly assembled track. Ben trails with another string of cars. They make chugging sounds with their mouths. Raina is stationed in the opposite corner, facing the computer while conversing softly on a Bluetooth earpiece—a recently acquired accessory that suits an art director, though not a middle-aged union lawyer. Ben stands up when he hears me enter, but then opts for the trains and sits back down. Frank waves politely.

For a minute I remain in the hallway, hesitant to disturb the tranquil scene playing out in my living room, when for a second time today, I catch Frank's gaze and again find it to be ever-so-slightly drawn out.

"I think I'll maybe catch a few winks before dinner," I announce.

First I linger in front of an open refrigerator. It's more barren than I recall. Reminds me of how my own fridge looked pre-marriage. Three stouts capped with gold foil, a house present from one of Raina's new co-workers, are lined up in the door. The allure of good beer.

For the record, I am by no stretch an alcoholic, recovering or otherwise, nor has that label ever been pinned on me (despite a healthy familial legacy). I simply choose to abstain. I find the interference of booze upon the life of a hardworking, morally driven man to be unnecessary. To deny, though, that alcohol was involved on the final night of my very first union conference in Phoenix many years ago, spent in the company of Lily, a colleague from Athens, Georgia, which nearly cost me my marriage, would be disingenuous. Thus, my abstinence must also be viewed as a symbolic pact with my wife and with myself, representing the closure of our relationship's most bitter and now unspoken chapter.

I ought to seize my chance, before Frank goes, to rest in solitude. Raina and I share, with our son, the apartment's only bedroom. But I stand in front of the open refrigerator a moment longer. I could, after all this time, have a beer if I wanted to, without doing harm. And then there's the bottle of Johnny Walker Black, a gift from an appreciative union rep, collecting dust in the back of the cabinet above the fridge. But now, for obvious reasons, is not the time.

To be welcoming, I ask Frank if he wants one. He deliberates. The trains stop. From the opposite end of the room, Raina, who'd seemed lost in work, pivots her head in my direction. Somehow my question has been understood as a trick, a test requiring a correct response.

"Or anything else?" I offer. "Seltzer, juice, water?"

"I want juice, Daddy."

"How do you say it nicely?" Frank asks Ben.

"Daddy, I want juice, please."

"I'll take some water," Frank says. "Thanks."

"Daddy, I want water."

* * *

IT'S MY NINTH BIRTHDAY. My father is cajoling me to go on the ride. The sun bakes my forearms, ankles, and the tops of my sandaled feet. I'm soaked in sweat. My stomach feels queasy from the overload of greasy snacks my dad had intended as a treat. My head swarms with the foreign sights and sounds of men and women and their kids whose likes I've never before encountered. Their shrieks and laughter merge with the din of the rides thudding over our heads, and with the hucksters' ceaseless calls, beckoning one and all to their booths. The crowd presses us forward until we're at the front: The Coney Island Cyclone.

* * *

"LONG DAY?" RAINA ASKS me.

It's dark out now, and it's just the two of us on the couch, talking and sipping mugs of ginger tea. Ben is on the floor engrossed in his nightly screening of *Dumbo*. In the past, the length of most feature-length films and their penchant for digression and emotive imagery, in place of a directly linear narrative, had proven problematic for him. When a character sat around for too long thinking, or a nonsensical moment occurred, he didn't become bored so much as confused, asking questions like, *What's he doing?* But since Raina's best friend, Cal, gave him the *Dumbo* DVD for his third birthday, he's doggedly stuck to the film, viewing it night after night with Zen-like concentration. He seems genuinely moved by the love between the mother elephant and her son, and I know he further desires to understand the film on every level.

"Yeah," I say, "It was a long day." My body's unintended expressions are always giving me away. I mean, I know Raina well after twenty-one years, but with her it's as if she sees me from the inside. She can always tell. "I had this meeting in the morning," I continue, "everything felt long after that."

What was amazing was that Raina knew instantly about my feelings for Jessie just by the way I brought her up. She practically knew before I did. Raina told me she confirmed her suspicions when she saw how I acted with Jessie at last year's office Christmas party.

"Meeting with the partners or a client?" she asks.

She leans back against the arm of the couch. Raina didn't even get mad about the Christmas party. *What's there to be mad about?* she'd said.

"Actually, neither. The new union rep from Allied Health Employees asked me earlier in the week if I'd meet personally with one of their members who'd lost her job. See if I thought she had a case. The catch was the union had only until this weekend to file a grievance and still be timely under the contract. I told them to file it anyway to be sure it gets in on time."

"What happens, again, when they're late?"

"When they're late?" There was a time in our marriage when Raina had a better grasp on the tenets of labor law. Maybe she's just distracted by the new procedures and personalities at her job. Or our new babysitter. "Well, nothing good. The boss will refuse to consider the grievance, and the union member will be furious. Once a worker isn't protected under contract, the employer can't be held responsible."

"Right." Raina sips her tea.

"Anyway," I say, "this woman comes into the office today all the way from Coney Island. She's one of those people who exudes a certain quality that lets you know they've had it rough, you know?"

"Sure."

"She was about your age. Maybe younger. Mid-to-late thirties, I guess. And she was pleasant looking. Well, sort of. I mean, she should've been. All her features were pleasant, but her face expressed too many problems to be just that. Anyway, her appearance isn't what's important. There was something about her—"

"Mommy," Ben calls. Raina motions for me to hold my thought while she attends to him. Ben can't control his need to interrupt regularly to confirm that we're still paying attention. He has a question about why Dumbo is seeing pink elephants. He's asked each of us a hundred times before. Now the answer comes included in his question. "Because he drank the bad stuff the clowns put in his bucket?" he asks and proclaims simultaneously.

Raina kneels down and drapes her arms around his tiny chest. She's taken off her workwear, and now, in her post-dinner attire—a worn white v-neck—her breasts, braless, envelop his face. At strange moments and all varieties of circumstance, I sometimes catch myself muting the particular episode in front of me and undressing Raina with my eyes: short; thick in the center and thighs; full, protruding chest; slightly asymmetrical face; large bright hazel eyes that tilt at different degrees; a rounded nose that comes to a sharp point; a tangle of dirty-blonde curls; firm, ruddy, radiant skin.

She kisses Ben and returns to the couch.

"So tell me about the case."

"So this woman—her name is Doreen—she was fired in the first week of August for an incident that took place in July. She was a receptionist at a health clinic in Brooklyn, a small place on Mermaid Avenue in Coney Island. Now, Doreen claims she takes it upon herself to know everyone who comes into the clinic, to remember their face as well as their medical status. She said she'd found that after so many years in her field, she was able to recognize a patient's problem, almost without fail, from the moment they stepped in the door."

"She told you this?" Raina says.

"Yeah. It's bizarre. Essentially she claims to have earned an on-the-job, extrasensory medical degree. She described the gait of the alcoholic, the fidgeting of a crack addict, the schizophrenic's shifting stare. But most prominent, she said, is the abuse victim. She says she sees them everywhere, on the subway, walking down the street, and that they haunt her daily."

"Whoa," Raina says.

"I know," I say, shifting in my seat. "So, while we have no documentation from the clinic yet, Doreen is convinced that the complaint against her came from a woman named Olga Petrova, someone Doreen grew up with in Jackson Heights. Olga came in one day looking to see a physician. The two of them hadn't seen each other since childhood, but Doreen recognized Olga immediately and took it upon herself to try to help her old friend be seen as soon as possible. And get this: she said she could tell right away that Olga was a victim of abuse."

"What did she do?" Raina asks, "Doreen—did she say something to her?"

"Apparently she was only sympathetic. She said she knew better than to confront her about it, but I guess she got pretty frustrated when she couldn't help get Olga immediate attention, and she told Olga as much. When Doreen came in the following Monday, she was told she'd violated a patient's rights, that she'd breached confidentiality and used threatening and hostile language that profoundly upset the patient. And she was terminated."

* * *

THE IMPASSIONED NOISE OF my son's protests sputter angrily against a stream of his sobs. Dumbo and his mother are already reunited, and the train sailed off into the sunset. The End. Raina is once again holding Ben, and consequently subduing and quieting him as quickly as he starts. She tells Ben about his big day tomorrow. She tells him that if he cooperates, he can get two bedtime stories.

"Daddy's going to read to you tonight."

He gets about halfway to the bathroom and breaks down again.

"You can watch the movie again tomorrow. Now it's time to relax and get ready for bed. How about Daddy reads one story to you, then I read one to you?"

We're perpetually compromising with Ben. It's fitting that the son of a lawyer should already have internalized at the age of three that there is no such thing as an unbreakable rule or an unalterable situation. Thus far his only negotiating strategy is to cry. And it's effective.

"It's okay," I say. "You guys read tonight. Can I read to you tomorrow night, Ben?" He stares at me blankly. "I'll take that as a yes. I love you." I walk over and steal a kiss from his wet cheek.

Once Raina and Ben disappear into the bedroom, I turn on the TV. I retrieve my briefcase and lay Doreen's file out on the coffee table. Raina's voice creeps in from the other room as she starts to read. I turn off the overhead light and lie down on the couch.

Other than the news and the occasional Ken Burns PBS special, I haven't watched much TV in years. But, rather than feeling superior to the newer wave of sitcoms and the reality shows, I actually feel quite old and dumb when I watch them. Similar to Ben's relationship with *Dumbo*, there's a dimension to the shows that I don't understand. Yet my curiosity isn't sparked like his. The editing and shaky camerawork feels so distracting that I often lose track of what's at stake. How about making a show where a family all sleeps in the same room so nobody has a sex life? Maybe it's already been done. I switch the TV off.

Suddenly, I'm seeing Doreen seated across my desk, shrinking downward, her thin neck lowering over her already-hunched shoulders. I picture her entrance into my office. First, Robin's voice over the intercom, *A Ms. Grant is here to see you, Tom.* And that sound of footsteps in the corridor that signifies the imminent presence of a brand new other inside my office. And then this woman—deathly pale, bleach blonde, lightly freckled, blue-gray eyes—wearing a dress that seems to belong to a different era.

I picture the vacant expression Doreen must have worn on her walk home from her former job that August morning, not even a half hour after arriving. I don't remember much after that. I felt numb. Nothing made sense. It didn't seem real. She said it wasn't until she returned home and saw her husband, Hunter, asleep in their bed, that she went into her living room and cried. She said she cried for a month, and was despondent for nearly another before contacting the union. Prior to that she'd felt too crushed to do anything.

"Did she have any idea how close she came to exceeding the sixty-day time frame for pursuing grievances in the contract?" Jessie had asked me over coffee. "She wouldn't have had a case at all."

My apartment is silent. I close my eyes and discover the familiar, muted hum of taxis whirring around Union Square and the cry of ambulances rushing victims to St. Vincent's.

I wonder what Doreen's doing at this moment. Maybe she's alone right now. At home in Coney Island in some shitty flat with cheap furniture.

Raina tiptoes into the living room, sits on the couch and sighs. I listen to her breathe.

She's drowsy, or at least believes she is, and in another minute will start either to vent her frustrations with work or with her mother or with Cal's latest flame, or pass out on my shoulder.

I kiss her.

Then, taking her under her arms, I lean her across the couch. I unbutton her jeans and tug them down her legs, over her ankles. Raina's hands instinctively shield her crotch. Her thighs quiver from the sudden exposure to the air. A few days' hair growth on her legs doesn't faze me anymore.

"Tom," she says softly. "I'm not..." But she doesn't finish, and I kiss her.

I grasp her wrists, lift her arms over her head and attempt to warm her by covering her with my clothed body. She moans upon impact. I hold her wrists with one of my hands and push my free hand, fingers out, between her legs until she's ready. Then I undress.

I brush her hair back from her face. Her complacency makes me go harder until she starts breathing audibly loud and quick. It's been a while and I feel good. I go faster and harder. When Raina gets too loud, I put my finger gently to her lips. She bites it. She digs her nails into my hips.

"Stop."

"What?"

"Mommy?"

Ben is standing timorously at the other end of the room, lips pouted, chin over chest, milk-distended belly out against outer space pajamas.

"Ben," I say.

"Hi, my love," Raina says.

My reaction is to lie deeper into Raina and wrap my arms around her to conceal myself and show Ben that his parents are hugging. But Raina pushes me off.

She hurries to Ben and picks him up, naked legs and all. "Were you having trouble sleeping?" They disappear into the bedroom.

In the bathroom, I run a cool shower, finish myself off, and brush my teeth. I enter the bedroom as Raina's leaving.

"Ben is going to sleep."

"Okay," I say. "Me too."

I kiss Ben and slide into my bed.

"Is that you, Daddy?"

"Yup."

"Are you going to sleep now with me?"

"Uh-huh."

"Is Mommy coming to bed?"

"Soon."

"I love you, good night."

"I love you too. Sweet dreams."

2

I wake to stripes of gray-blue light that bleed filtered and dulled through the slatted shade by our bed. Raina sleeps on the other side of me, closer to Ben.

It's early, but not so early that it will be long before Ben is up and tugging on Raina's weary body, wanting first to be held, then craving a minute later cartoons and toys, all the while requiring cereal and fresh clothes before nursery school.

To ensure that I have no part in disrupting Raina's rest, I carefully shimmy down the length of our bed, as I often do, and slink past Ben's low-lying, perpendicular bed. Ben, a sizable pool of drool on his pillow, is asleep on his stomach holding Elmo with one arm.

Toys congest the living-room floor. Raina and I make a point to tidy the apartment every Sunday, but by Friday, inevitably, something's getting in my way. Train tracks snake along the carpet. Matchbox cars and a fire engine are parked in front of the couch. I imagine stepping on one of Ben's favorite toys, perhaps splintering the plastic rooftop of the fire engine with my heel. They'd hate me for it.

With my face lathered and white, I bring the razor to my cheek. Doreen's bony, troubled face flickers for a moment in the steamed glass. The razor catches on my skin, just below my jaw. A trickle of red.

* * *

N TRAIN TO TIMES Square: the station is alive, people crossing in every direction at different rhythms. Up ahead, underneath the Lichtenstein mural, a flautist and a bongo player are heads down, playing some kind of jazz. I take a dollar from my wallet and watch the bill's jerky descent into the wicker basket below.

On the street, I stop to watch a small crew lugging half-kegs through the front door of the Times Square Brewery. Two guys smoke cigarettes, dressed in all white—kitchen staff, most likely.

At my desk. The spring-loaded arm of my draftsman lamp has crept, once again, imperceptibly down during the night. I angle it back and watch the circle of yellow light spread like a rising sun across the landscape. Mountains of print, transcripts, communications, depositions, and decisions—old and new, finished and unfinished, both loose and bound in a plethora of styles befitting the time and taste of the clerks, lawyers, and secretaries involved—offer a rough representation of my day, my week, my month, my career.

My latest litigation involves Elena Gomez, a public school teacher who was abruptly fired last month when her social security number came back "no match." This, after six years of employment plus another ten in the private sector.

"It's the number I've always used," she'd said. "The one my father told me was mine. It's never been a problem. Why now?"

Elena, who was born in the DR and raised in the Bronx, is the ninth separate "no match" case our office has handled in the last year. Sudden pressure from the brute and clumsy hand of our post-9/11 government.

At noon, the office gathers around the long table in the conference room for lunch. On the walls hang framed posters of César Chávez, Samuel Gompers, John Steinbeck, Martin Luther King Jr., and Rosie the Riveter. We can do it. I sit at one end with the senior partners and the secretaries, and Jessie and the younger lawyers congregate at the other.

My firm is blessed with some of the sharpest minds and the most idealistic hearts of a generation. Sure, a few years back we lost two Harvard grads to corporate law, the dark side, as we referred to it, but that's always gone on. The atmosphere that remains here is one of empathy, hard work, and a keen and worldly intellect. Today there's a lot of talk of Bush's recent nomination of Judge John Roberts for the Supreme Court. It's disheartening news to an office full of dyed-in-the-wool progressives, but I actually think it makes us dig our heels in and fight harder.

With ample experience behind me and with relative youth by lawyer standards, I have, in all likelihood, entered my professional prime. If this firm were a sports team, I think my partners would agree—assuming they were alright with that metaphor—I'd be captain. According to the firm's revenue earned minus expenses incurred,

I'd also be the leading scorer. Forty-six for lawyers may be what twenty-six is to a ball player.

There are three senior partners who've been on the payroll since I joined the firm. They're like elders at a holiday feast. Each aging lefty still retains a nicely furnished office, but since they make an appearance only a few days a week, as breadwinners they've been on the decline for years. It was common knowledge that Bernie Levan, who commuted from the Hamptons, wasn't even breaking even. In a week he was headed south for a little Florida R&R. But for better or worse, they're still buddies with some of our largest clients, having garnered national reputations, and comprise the firm's namesake: Cunningham, Klein, and Levan. No one is in a position to move them out the door, and their presence at holiday parties and client-sponsored conferences involving golf and free dinners, which incidentally, they never seem to miss, is strangely comforting. At least to me it is. My father died my first year away from home so I find solace in three regal, slow-moving men, their slumped shoulders, liver-spotted scalps, and spongy midsections.

I've always had a particular fondness for John Cunningham, a tall, brilliant, dignified seventy-four-year-old born in Manchester, who smokes a pipe against building regulations and doctor's orders and wears argyle sweaters and a Welsh hunting jacket in the fall. He has the classic good looks of a former leading man. He's lived in the Village since the sixties and has a wealth of inspiring, crass tales, which are good for morale.

In part, I like John because I've long suspected that he'd advocated for me when I was hired, just two years out of law school. For unclear reasons, Cunningham seemed to be of the opinion that I was some kind of legal mastermind—an old-school scholar. From the beginning he made a regular point to consult me on legal niceties and nuances that veered toward the philosophical. Also, in those early days, he used to invite me on Friday afternoons to lunch at the Italian restaurant under the Edison Hotel. He'd feed me drinks and expound ideas on esoteric legal matters over spaghetti and clam sauce. Just me and one of the most highly esteemed labor lawyers in Manhattan. When I gave up drinking, I largely gave up Friday lunches with John. I went twice more, and to his credit he didn't act hurt when I declined gin and tonic, but it wasn't the same. I never blamed Raina for this. It was, like

I said, my decision. John and I remain friendly. Occasionally he forgets and offers me a cocktail in the late afternoon, so I know he keeps a bottle somewhere in his office.

On this Friday afternoon, John is still out of the office, visiting his forty-year-old son, who not long ago began a third tenure at a rehab clinic in Tucson. I don't hang around and talk after lunch, but take some water back to my office, check my email, and find myself waiting for three o'clock.

* * *

"IT'S FUNNY," I SAY. "I never thought I'd be a regular at a place like this."

"Oh yeah?" says Jessie. We're standing in line at Dunkin' Donuts on the corner of Broadway and 45th.

"Well, I used to go to the Starbucks up the street if I wanted an afternoon coffee. But that was only on rare occasions."

"They got you with the trendy music, huh?"

I grin helplessly.

"I wouldn't take you for the type to support Dunkin' Donuts," she says. Jessie is a twenty-four-year-old law student we hired on as a part-time legal assistant at the firm last fall. "They don't exactly set a gleaming example for labor relations, do they?"

"Starbucks, Dunkin' Donuts, they all have miserable records when it comes to accepting the right of workers to organize."

"I guess you're right."

"It's the uninterrupted trend in the history of big business," I say. "Truthfully, we shouldn't patronize either, but it's like, look around you—any semblance of a mom and pop operation has long since gone the way of the hardware store and the peep show." I hand Grace, our regular cashier, six dollars, which gets two medium coffees and a cruller and leaves a twenty percent tip. "And then there's the convention of the tip: a compensatory system I'm also ideologically against, but of course practice, for the reason that I'm not a complete asshole."

Now she's the one grinning. Fridays are casual at the office and Jessie wears a pinstriped, navy blue dress. It leaves her long neck exposed, the two delicate diagonal tendons alongside the trachea, and a hint of collarbone. I'm in a suit sans tie. We find a table in the back.

"You look overworked," I say, which is true, although she looks utterly good to me. Jessie has these big wet eyes. Water eyes.

"Yeah. My weekend began prematurely. An old friend's in town."

"Guy or girl?"

"A guy." Jessie says. "He's staying with me too."

"In that tiny apartment in Williamsburg?" I say. I've gripped my cup too forcefully and a small spurt of scalding coffee has overflowed onto my knuckles, though Jessie doesn't seem to notice. I wince in private pain.

"That's where I live," she says. "Anyway, Tyler's an old friend from home. While I'm happy to see him, it's been a lot having him around when I've got studying and classes in the afternoon and work in the morning. You know how old friends can be."

I nod and dry my knuckles against my palm.

"I promised him we'd go out in Manhattan tonight. We're going to meet after work and wander toward Chelsea."

Maybe Jessie's considerate disposition is the byproduct of a solid Midwestern upbringing. Maybe she's just young. Either way, Jessie seems to possess an uncanny ability to say or do precisely what people want, when she wants to.

"It'll be funny being a tour guide after being here just a short while," Jessie muses, "but by my very first visit home, everyone had already dubbed me a New Yorker."

Jessie's from an old farming town in Nebraska. In college, she was a classics major as well as a cyclist, the latter being a topic I haven't probed too deeply but have a natural admiration for. I used to be a runner.

"I know what you mean," I say. "I've lived here my whole life and it still feels odd to show other people where I live. It's as though when they ask for a tour or to be shown a good time, they're implicitly asking, *so what makes your life here so special?*"

I put my hand on my neck to scratch an itch and feel the cut from my earlier shaving mishap.

"Do you want to get a drink?" I say.

"Now?" she says. "We're drinking coffee."

"Right, I don't mean this instant. I walk by that brewery on 42nd every day. I've been meaning to try it. Plus, you and I have never had a drink together. I mean a real drink."

"I thought you didn't do that."

"Didn't do what? Drink? I don't—or I didn't. I can though."

She looks at me quizzically.

"I wanted to talk about the Allied Health Employees case. I'm meeting with the receptionist, Doreen, next week before I draft up my settlement proposal. If the clinic doesn't bite I want to get the arbitration on track as soon as possible. There's no reason to drag this thing out."

She appears on the verge of speaking but then hesitates. I have a golden opportunity to rescind my offer with a simple excuse, offending no one and swiftly righting the situation. All memory of the invitation for drinks could soon be largely forgotten and—

"Alright," she says.

"Alright what?"

"Alright, I want that drink. But I need to finish organizing some trial exhibits for Margaret back at the office. Then I'll come find you."

* * *

I DRUM MY DESK with my fingers. Still no word back from the Coney Island Health Clinic. It's been over a week since I'd faxed them a letter requesting a copy of any report produced from their investigation into Doreen's alleged misconduct. It was standard practice for an employer to turn it over.

Doreen was born in Jackson Heights and never lived outside of Queens. It was in Queens that she became passionate about working at health clinics. It was also in Queens that she started to memorize the conditions of all the patients. The promotion to billing and records gave her unlimited access to everyone's charts.

She had an ex-husband in Jackson Heights who worked up the street at an auto body shop. On the surface, it didn't seem relevant. But she claimed he was the reason she left her first job and moved to Coney Island. Once she remarried, she didn't like knowing her ex-husband was so close.

And then there was Olga: the miraculous reappearance of a childhood friend. Seeing Olga's bruised condition had devastated Doreen. If Olga had been mistreated—and Doreen was certain that this was the case—then her injuries demanded immediate attention. According to Doreen, Dr. Kaplan, the head physician at the clinic, hadn't agreed. This enraged her.

Raina was expecting me to arrive home on the early side tonight. Next to the computer monitor is a photograph of Raina in her late twenties, posing by a willow tree in the Brooklyn Botanical Gardens. Next to that is a picture I took last Thanksgiving of Raina cradling Ben, flanked by my mother and sister. I take the phone from the receiver and then set it back down. I pick up the phone again and dial Raina.

* * *

IT'S 4:30 P.M. AND I'm roaming the hallways. What should I drink tonight? Whiskey? No. I should go easy. I head to the small office kitchen and fill a cup of water from the cooler. As I turn around I find myself face-to-face with Margaret, the firm's newest straight-to-partner ace.

"Just the man I'm looking for." Margaret says. Margaret is a seasoned Winnipeg transplant that the firm picked up just two falls ago. Her mid-life decision to trade in her quaint-but-respectable government job in Manitoba for a Times Square office and a high-rise flat with her girlfriend on the Upper East Side had been our serendipitous good fortune. "The partners are dining at Molvydos after work with the intention of talking shop, most notably what our Christmas bonuses are looking like for this year."

"Tonight?"

"That's the plan. Are you busy? We could reschedule for a night you're free."

"No, no, if I'm the only one holding everyone up, you should carry on without me. I have plans. With Raina—my wife. How about you call me later this weekend to fill me in?"

"Sure. I'll have to drink extra for you." Margaret winks.

Apparently she's unaware of my reputation as a teetotaler.

"Sounds good," I say.

My sights fix down the hall on the wine-colored finish of Cunningham's office door. I spot his secretary Donna's ring of keys dangling from a hook behind her desk. The sound of her animated laughter emanates from the copy room down the hall. I reach over, take the keys, unlock Cunningham's door, drop them back on the hook, and slip inside.

The room is fantastically black. It's noiseless. Donna's laughter, the hum of the copy machine, the clacking of keyboards, the ring of the phones and fax machines have stopped. I reach out and feel the client's chair. For over forty years, the working class men and women of the metropolis have come, from nearly every organized profession, to sit and tell John how they've been mistreated by their superiors. My hand follows the contour of his desk. I sit in John's revolving chair. It's worn on the left arm.

Posturing there, my eyes slowly adjust. From depthless black, the outlines of the room exhibit softer shades, deep blue and purple. I open the top drawer of his desk and feel over pencils, pens, rulers, a Zippo. I go to his bookcase and run my hand along the backs of every shelf, behind all the volumes of laws and regulations. I probe around the coat rack, the umbrella stand, under the curtains. On the end of the windowsill stands a globe tilted at thirty degrees on a bronze base with a bare-breasted goddess emerging out of the North Pole. The equator is a thick, black strip with a sliver of steel running through the middle. Placing a hand on the base, and another around the goddess, I pull. The globe splits easily open on rear hinges revealing a bottle of Tanqueray. The neighboring compartment stores a martini glass.

I pour a few fingers worth into the glass and saddle up next to it on the windowsill. Times Square, the brightly lit circus, is churning on 7th Avenue. I lied to Raina and then to the partners, telling each of them I had plans with the other when really I'll be getting drinks with Jessie. Deception hadn't figured into any of this. The lies had simply come out, almost smoothly, with very little hesitation. Things are becoming shady, but I'm not yet guilty of anything. I raise my glass in the darkness and drink.

The old burn. Vicious, toxic, cleansing. Pure gin—never my drink—striking, as if to pierce through the stomach's lining, before firing back up through the throat, filling the sinuses with its hard-to-place, bitter vapors, and exiting the body behind reddened, watery eyes, leaving the brain adrift inside a liquid skull.

Nervous moments ensue. I see my son's small hand wrapped over my finger and the top of his head as he toddles below me, while Raina squats, at the other end of the living room, arms wide. Then Lily, inserting and reinserting her keycard, until a square light above the lock turns green and the door opens in.

I down the rest of the glass. This time, when the gin settles, I feel calmer. I pour another, but don't touch it right away. Then the door handle turns. I remain still as someone enters and the door shuts.

"Tom?"

I clear my throat.

"I finished my work and I've been looking all over for you," Jessie says, coming closer. Her voice is sweet and cool.

"What're you doing in here?" She puts a blind hand out and finds my wrist. She holds it a moment and regains her balance. "You smell like alcohol."

"I cheated," I say. "Started early. Want one?"

She accepts the glass, sniffs the gin, and takes what amounts to a negligible sip.

"Cunningham's stash," I say.

Earlier at Dunkin' Donuts, I'd ended things by telling her about how it used to be with Cunningham and me: Friday afternoon gin-and-tonics at the Edison back in the old days. I retrieved for her a forgotten story about a time we'd tailed a suspicious looking man, Columbo-style, all the way to the East River where he passed off one of two identical briefcases before leading us back to our very building where he'd gotten off on the 17th floor, to be spotted at various times over the next year before disappearing. Jessie was all smiles. I'd succeeded in stamping the occurrence of drinks between a senior lawyer and an aspiring lawyer as a reputable and exclusive tradition, one which she might join.

"Sorry there's no chaser."

She takes a longer sip, sputters, waits, and then, like me, gulps down the rest.

"Whoa," she says, bringing her wrist to her mouth. A rectangle of white teeth breaks from the shadows. "Can we go now?"

* * *

The Times Square Brewery, as it turns out, may be the most sanitized bar on the planet. The drinkers are hoarded together to one side around a long, black, S-shaped counter. A barkeep in black button-down and tie is handling orders. I'm trapped between two wide-backed business types and a swarthy goateed man smiling at a woman in a lime, stretchy miniskirt.

"Let's go upstairs." Jessie says. I nod and follow. Blood rushes to my head. The gin.

The second floor is more tables. It's as sterile as a hospital cafeteria.

The third floor, strangely enough, is carpeted in mauve, reminiscent of holidays spent in my grandparents' living room on Long Island. At one end of the floor is a square bar with a female bartender dressed identically to the one downstairs. A sheer glass wall shows off the piping and stainless steel vats where the house drafts are brewed.

I order the pilsner and Jessie gets a German beer called Dunkel. Pint in hand, I turn to Jessie who, unceremoniously, has already begun imbibing, so I peer once, straight through the suds to the bottom of my glass, and swallow. The beer is crisp and delicious, even more so than I remembered. I can't peel my gaze from Jessie. Her body in profile, a brand new angle for me, mesmerizes.

I take another swig; then I'm talking. She looks straight at me with those reflective eyes. I've started without knowing what I'm saying until I start hearing myself. It's as if I'm making a long-distance phone call with a two-second delay. I'm going on about my days in law school, how nervous I was about the bar. She's looking at me, laughing occasionally. Really we're gushing.

At some point she turns to me, brushing my calf, intentionally or not, while resting her feet on the rung of my stool.

"Another round?" I ask.

"I better start heading back to the office. Tyler should be here soon."

I make a quarter turn to her, lowering my hand toward her thigh, before dropping it in my own lap.

She smiles. I feel myself blushing.

On the stairs, she squeezes my hand and then lets it go before we reach the lobby.

Outside, the circus is in full swing, the sky an indefinite orange. Neon colors illuminate her face. The sun is probably in the middle of setting but it makes no difference under the skyscrapers and billboards.

We're crossing over 8th Avenue, a short sprint from the office when I catch her hand, step into an alcove, and pull her toward me. Her tongue moves aggressively over mine. Then she slows—a moment of softness before it's over.

Back on 44th, we're sitting on stone stairs a few buildings from the office.

"You like it here?" I say. "At the firm?"

"Yeah, of course I like it. It's a great firm."

"Do you want to work on this next case with me?"

"The lady at the health clinic?"

"Doreen," I say.

"Oh, look. There he is," she says.

Tyler's too far to discern us in the dusk. I press my lips against the base of her neck. But she doesn't react.

Tyler's a baby-faced guy in tight, brand new jeans. Jessie greets him with a kiss on the cheek.

"Tyler, this is Tom," she says. "Tom's my boss. We're working on a case together."

Tyler and I shake hands and with a wave they start off. I sit back down and watch them go. It's my direction too, but I don't want to leave just yet. The old warmth is rising over me like waves.

3

There's rustling in my bed.
"Oh no. Baby..."

I turn over and see Raina carting Ben out of the room. It's wet beneath my hand. The scent of urine.

5:32 A.M. I'm awake. And I feel remarkably good. To evade the puddles Ben has left on Raina's side, I slither, crab-like, down the length of the bed as if her body were still lying there.

I pull off our blanket and wrench the sheets and the pillowcases. Ben's bed is damp and I strip it too. I gather everything, stuff it into a laundry bag, and go about making the beds with fresh sheets, tucking them in hospital corners the way my dad taught me. He learned in the army. I prop Elmo up next to Ben's pillow.

I expect to find Ben soaking in a bath, but he's kneeling on the bathmat in his little robe, already squeaky clean, hair parted, babbling nonsensically and directing an interaction between a pirate and a dolphin on the lip of the tub while watching his mother shower through a part in the curtain. Eyes closed, head back, her sturdy body gleams beneath the rush of water, indifferent to our presence.

"Off to the laundromat," I say.

I kissed my assistant. I kissed Jessie. Or we kissed each other. Already it seems a peculiar memory, thrilling and distant.

* * *

BY ELEVEN A STEADY rain rules out a trip to the Central Park Zoo. Raina reads the *Times* and Ben crawls in circles with his firetruck. WKCR plays softly from the radio in the kitchen. A dull pressure in my head undermines my efforts to concentrate, and gradually my morning vigor evaporates like an untended pot of boiling water.

At half past noon, I tell Raina she should go out if she wants while I stay and put Ben down for his nap. Ben is too tired to protest after his untimely shock into wakefulness this morning, and is actually grateful to have one of us lie with him.

After sending Ben on a forced trip to the toilet, we lie down on his short, freshly made bed and I read to him from *The Polar Express*. He's asleep before the train makes it to the North Pole. I'm tired too, but it's too cramped for me to sleep and my mind continues to churn.

I gaze at my son's handsome face: a mop of dark brown hair, a thin upturned nose, a dimpled chin. Six months ago, he'd been red complexioned, chubby in the cheeks and under the neck, but overnight it seemed the baby-fat had fallen away and he'd emerged, like a tulip bulb from beneath a winter frost, a knockout. Three-year-olds are cute, particularly in the eyes of their progenitors, but Ben stopped traffic. I can't recall a subway ride where he hasn't been the recipient of lavish praise. Frank reports the same. It's hard to say what exactly is so appealing about his appearance. But there it is: a universal charm. Ben's a natural with a crowd. Cal sees profit and counsels Raina on starting him in modeling and acting. I've tried to picture my son in a Pull-Ups commercial. All those smiling children on TV have to belong to somebody.

I fix on his eyes. His eyes are mine.

My mind stumbles on last night's walk home. Ninth Avenue glows and sways with the novelty of Friday-night New York. Snarling, shiny-eyed faces realized by drink and privilege. The windows of cabs, limos, sports bars, chic eateries.

I'd paused in the entryway of my building, staring into the antique mirror. Music was spilling out of one of the units upstairs. This was a rarity ever since Raina and I'd been grandfathered into our rent-stabilized one-bedroom apartment in one of the tamer buildings on the block. Her father, Dr. Stoltz, a professor of urban planning at NYU, had put her on the lease before retiring to a nursing home in Connecticut.

It turned out the music was coming from our place. The Beatles maybe. As I climbed the stairs, laughter and stomping joined the mix. I peered through the peephole in the front door.

Ben danced into view. He was naked and twisting wildly, mimicking the break-dancers he'd seen in Union Square. Then Frank's slight figure. He too was naked, save for a pair of boxer-briefs. I was shocked and momentarily frozen. Things looked bizarre and sinister in a way that's hard to explain. My right hand balled into a fist tight enough to ache. What was he doing here? And where was Raina? But then Frank disappeared and returned with pajamas, which he waved coaxingly in front of Ben.

"I don't want to get dressed," my son moaned.

"Sorry," said Frank, hitting pause on the stereo, "but you're going to catch cold. We can't start the music again until you put on your pajamas."

Ben started to cry, but it wasn't one of those deep cries. It was the same I'm-not-getting-just-what-I-want cry that gets me flustered because I know he's not going to listen to me.

But Frank held his ground. He said something like, "C'mon man, you gotta cooperate, I want to keep dancing too, but it's time to put on some clothes. I'm gonna put on mine. Then we can listen to two more songs before bed." Ben looked to his belly for a moment of reflection, before conceding, "Alriiiight," and allowing Frank to dress him.

Alright? I couldn't believe it. Ben never cooperates like that with me when I'm laboring to get him out the door in the morning. Not that quickly. Frank was good. Really good.

I saw for the first time that Ben's hair was wet. My son didn't like to wear clothes after a bath. Frank had stripped down for bath time so Ben wouldn't soak his clothes with all the splashing. I often did the same.

I let myself in the house while Frank was dressing.

"You go away!" Ben said when he saw me.

It turned out Raina had phoned Frank last minute. She was probably getting drunk somewhere with Cal.

I let Frank put Ben to bed and then paid him. When he was gone, I dug out the Johnny Walker from the back of the liquor cabinet, twisted off the plastic seal, took a swig, and put it back.

* * *

THE RAIN'S PICKED UP, audibly thumping the lids of the trashcans in the courtyard. I crawl over Ben and leave him to sleep.

In the past, September weekends meant catching an early train to Raina's childhood home where her mom would serve up a hearty lunch; after which, like two teenagers, we'd borrow the Subaru for an unmapped spin through brilliant-hued Hudson Valley where we'd hike a mountain, drink a bottle of local wine, fuck like bunny rabbits, sleep at a B&B or else in Raina's tent, fuck some more, pick six bags of apples, drop off the car, and return home in time to dish out dinners at the Holy Apostle Soup Kitchen. Though ostensibly our excuse for not venturing north this fall will be our three-year-old and Raina's new job, our last private getaway or act of community service precedes both boy and job.

On NY1, there's a report about the Transit Union's plan to renegotiate worker contracts with the MTA. Thousands of miles away, two ill-conceived wars are being fought. Meanwhile, New Orleans remains underwater.

There's an invitation in the mail for my high-school reunion.

I sink into the couch and listen to the quieter sound of the rain as it falls, leaking a steady sigh into the apartment.

October

1

Another Tuesday morning at Cunningham, Klein, and Levan. Doreen breezes into my office wearing a beige, fur-collared coat, a green shoulder bag, red pumps, and dark sunglasses.

"Mr. Claughlin, I'm so sorry I'm late. I know how important time is for you lawyers."

Doreen clutches the back of the client's chair a few feet from my desk. Her hands pink from the cold. Her nails are meticulous, cherry-red. She wears a gold band with a sizeable turquoise gem on her ring finger.

"I had quite a morning," she says. "We've had no hot water for a few days now. Then the sink started leaking, and I really wanted Hunter to attend to it before I left for Manhattan and the whole kitchen flooded, and—"

"Ms. Grant," I say.

"I've been preparing for this meeting for weeks," she says. Her eyes meet mine.

"Please," I say, "take off your coat and have a seat."

Jessie takes Doreen's coat and hangs it on a hook by the door.

"Such a pretty assistant," Doreen says. "You're so young. You look like you could be in school. That's a compliment."

"Actually, I am in school," Jessie says. "I'm about to finish my law degree."

"I assure you Ms. Engel is one of our sharpest minds," I say.

"Oh, I have no doubt about that," Doreen says.

The women shake hands and sit.

"First," I say. "Stop apologizing. I'm the union's lawyer. They've hired me to handle your case so my time is on their dime. Now, if you held up a judge or an arbitrator like this it would be a real problem. But today, we've got some work to do, so let's get to it, okay?"

Doreen and Jessie both nod.

"Okay," I continue. "We received a fax from the health clinic this morning explaining that they're not going to release any documentation from your termination."

"Really, what did they say?"

Jessie reads: "The Coney Island Health Clinic declines to produce any report made during the clinic's investigation into Doreen Grant's misconduct because such a report is confidential. The investigation was based on a complaint made by a patient for inappropriate and damaging comments made by Ms. Grant. The comments were not only personally damaging to the patient, but were also in breach of the patient's confidentiality and the clinic's own confidentiality policies. The hurtful comments were made in front of more than one of the clinic's employees who have verified the complaint. The CIHC is deeply committed to protecting the privacy of its patients and employees."

"Why would they do this?" Doreen says. "They're making it all up. Don't you see? They know they're wrong."

"You may be correct," I say. "Invariably, in a wrongful termination case, it's in the employer's interest to introduce proof that the termination was warranted. It seems to me their case will need to rely on either witness testimony or a sworn statement from the wronged patient corroborated by an eyewitness or third party. You can't fire a person purely on hearsay."

"But Mr. Claughlin, that's why I've been so blessed to have you as my lawyer," Doreen says.

"As I said, I represent the Federation of Allied Health Employees. As such, I'll do everything I can to determine whether the clinic had just cause to fire you."

"Attorney Claughlin and I are going to do our best," Jessie chimes in, "to make sure you get all the money you should've been earning paid back to you, and to insist your record is cleaned of any wrongdoing."

I glance at Jessie. I appreciate her optimism, but she's being presumptuous. She's practically promising a successful outcome to our grievant, which for obvious reasons, made especially clear to a parent of a toddler, is never a good idea.

"Oh, that's wonderful," Doreen says. She hesitates before continuing. "The thing is, Mr. Claughlin, I took the liberty of doing something. You said yourself at our first meeting that we might need other people to support my track record. You said that if things came down to a matter of my character I might need this. Well, at first it made me upset—the idea of having to defend my character. You must understand how seriously I take my job. That's just how I am. But then a few days after our meeting, I realized I had to quit moping around my house feeling sorry for myself. I had to do something, you know? So I went back to the clinic—"

"Doreen—"

"Don't worry, I didn't go inside. I camped out a few stores down on the corner of 18th Street. And from the corner I waited for patients from the clinic to walk by. Most of them said hello on their own and asked me what I was doing out in the cold. I told them what happened. So many of them were sympathetic. We've all been there, right? I asked a small favor from those who felt for me. I asked them to write letters on my behalf. I told them I could use their words to get hired back. And they did. People wrote beautiful words on my behalf. They really stood up for me, you know? They stood up for what's right. It made me feel good. Everyone was so nice."

From her bag Doreen pulls out a manila envelope and hands it to me. Inside are nine single-page letters addressed *To whom it may concern*. The first one reads: My name is Matthew Botnikov and I recently found out that Doreen

Grant is no longer working at the Coney Island Health Clinic. I was dismayed to learn this and I would like to relate a positive experience I had once because of Doreen.

"This is... excellent," I say.

"Mr. Claughlin," Doreen says, her eyes ablaze. "I want my job back."

* * *

2:00 P.M. ALONE IN my office. Raina's smiling at me next to the willow tree. The orange lilies match her skirt. That's why she'd chosen to pose there.

I find my mind wandering to Barbara Jeffries and Gail Hathaway. Barbara was the receptionist in the financial aid office at George Washington University, where I spent my first two years as an undergraduate. My dad died the first week of my second semester. A heart attack. My father was only fifty-seven and looked healthy, and was as smart and well-read as anyone I'd ever met. He was one of those guys that made it a point to read the *Times* every morning from cover to cover. He owned the neighborhood newsstand where he worked six days a week. Sundays found him in nothing but boxers and an undershirt, reading, scotch in hand, in a wooden rocking chair. I would lie on the floor with my comics and read next to him. They said it happened in his sleep.

Shortly after I returned from the funeral, a hazy week of my mom's tears and rehearsed condolences from well-wishers, I found out I hadn't been enrolled for my second semester. Somehow, through all the drama and unrest, my tuition payment had been overlooked. This meant that all of my classes were automatically dropped. That was how I met Barbara.

My first encounter with Barbara set the tone for our relationship. I didn't have an appointment. She demanded to see my school ID, a brand new security measure the school had adopted. Surely the school had mailed me the ID over the winter break. But they'd sent it to a home that was, for the time being at least, too wrecked to take notice, let alone make sure it got into my hands. For this I would need to travel to the Office of Security. Can't you just look up my name? This is ridiculous. Barbara was probably around 300 pounds and her voice sounded it. *Excuse me young man, I don't make the rules.*

The Office of Security was a dead end. I couldn't acquire a student ID because my registration was canceled. I couldn't make an appointment to register because I didn't have a student ID. It felt like an existential joke.

Barbara and I had gotten off on the wrong foot. Her adherence to the rules rendered her incapable of offering me any help. I had to get around her. I tried coming at odd hours, early in the morning, right before closing, at her lunch-break, but invariably she was seated at her post. Every time she saw me she would just shake her head. I hated her.

Our exchanges climaxed in one particularly dramatic scene when it came to light, the week before midterms, that my exams wouldn't be graded if my name wasn't in the grade book. I returned to her office, desperate.

"Barbara," I said gathering all the sympathetic charm I could muster, "please help me. I need to speak to someone immediately so that I can enroll in my classes before the midterms. It would really mean a lot to me." I hoped she wouldn't recognize the previous me, made-over now as this ingratiating gentleman. But she did.

"Why should I help you, young man? You've been quite rude to me every time you've come in here."

"Barbara," I said, setting my palms down on her desk. Then, without thinking, I was hoisting myself up and swinging my legs over her desk, skipping gently over its surface, one step onto a low file drawer, and onto the carpet. Then I broke into a run. I didn't stop until I reached Gail's office at the end of the hallway.

I let myself in, immediately confessing almost tearfully to Gail Hathaway, the director of financial aid. *Please help me, the receptionist out there is being impossible. I need to register for my financial aid. My father just died!* Sure enough, with a few graceful movements, Gail, who proved to be an exceedingly understanding and generous listener, sprang into action. She had the authority to make it happen. She made a phone call, pulled out a current student ID card, sans photo, from her top desk drawer, and even signed me up, right then and there, for a work-study job in the archive section of the library. When Barbara came huffing in, Gail smiled warmly and told her that everything was under control.

* * *

To Whom It May Concern:

When I suffered a work-related injury last year and found myself at the Coney Island Heath Clinic, Doreen Grant not only got me an appointment immediately, she was so kind as to let me know how best to file my claim with my insurance. Doreen informed me of the benefits of switching my provider to the CIHC and personally set me up with a great primary care physician. Doreen was always compassionate and very helpful and perhaps the only person I encountered with an optimistic outlook and an ear for my pain.

To not have Doreen working at the clinic is a huge loss. When I stopped seeing her there, I felt it was not my business to inquire about her absence. I assumed she had moved on for personal reasons. But when I learned that she had been let go for an indiscretion, I was shocked and angered. In my personal experience with Doreen and when I've seen her with others, she has always handled things with patience and fairness. Now that Doreen is gone I'm considering changing providers altogether.

Sincerely,

Boris Marks

AS JESSIE READS, A lock of dark, curly hair falls over her face, which she instinctively tucks behind her ear.

"I think that one's eloquent," she says.

We're working in Cunningham's office; he's away this week on a prestigious pro bono case. In an unprecedented move, Cunningham has extended an open invitation to Jessie to use his office any time he's away.

"I agree. I think we should get in touch with this one," I say. "'An ear for my pain.' It's nice." I glance at the duplicitous globe on the windowsill. Fading sunlight curls over the North Pole. The names of countries and oceans are written in an old fashioned typescript. The USSR is intact.

Jessie catches me eyeing the globe and smiles.

"It humbles you to think about people like Doreen," I say. "Even if she can act a bit nuts. She's so giving."

I feel Jessie standing over me. I look up. Her face flushes and she looks down at her feet.

"Tom," she says, placing a hand on my forearm just below the roll of my sleeve, "that's how I think about you. Not the being nuts part. The part about being giving."

We kiss. I place my hands on her hips and fight the impulse to unbutton her shirt.

* * *

THE WIND CUTS STRAIGHT through my dress shirt, wrapping my tie around my neck. I'm on the roof, sixty-two stories up at Cunningham, Klein, and Levan. As usual, my time up here is tinged with paranoia that security or the NYPD will discover my presence—*What the fuck are you doing up here?*—and arrest me, though it's never been enough to stop me from returning.

I watch two construction workers on a lower rooftop across the street carrying cinder blocks from one large pile to another a few yards away over a short wall. If Ben were here, he'd ask, *Cause why?*

They might be members of the Builders Service Union, one of my firm's oldest clients. These are the people I fight for. I'm the guy with the conviction and know-how to win them contractually binding rights, compensation, and security—what other kind of security exists? Time and again, I'm the guy who'll fight to get their jobs back in the regrettable but altogether too frequent instances when their livelihood falls subject to the whim of some toxic supervisor. That's me. I'm that guy.

I'm going to do the best I can for you, Doreen. Guilty or not, everyone deserves a second chance.

I close my eyes. The wind's died down.

2

N train to Union Square: rush hour crowds collide. Through the corridor, I follow a series of advertisements for Stolichnaya Vodka. I stride purposefully uptown along the eastern edge of the park. We're going to the circus tonight.

Doreen's arbitration is set for five weeks from today—the third Tuesday in November. I've argued before Norcross, a memorably thorough arbitrator, twice in the last few years, and though I've yet to determine his politics, he strikes me as an honest and fair-minded guy. Both times he ruled in my favor.

Raina, Frank, and Cal, who holds Ben against his chest, stand outside my building. Raina's holding a cigarette.

"Smoking?" I say.

"They're mine," Frank says, "I'm quitting."

Frank is modeling a fluorescent orange scarf and a black beanie. For a second I recall watching through the peephole, Ben and him dancing, all twirling hips and flopping hair.

"We're having a vice day," Cal says. "Ben started it. Even though he had birthday cake at school, we still let him have ice cream."

Ben, who's been playing with the collar of Cal's leather jacket, perks up at the mention of his name and ice cream. Undoubtedly, he'll want more junk at the show.

"So Frank and I are having a cigarette, and Cal got the shoes he's been eyeing." Raina says, winking at me.

"And socks with gold toes," Ben says.

"Right," says Raina.

"Good memory," says Cal. He strokes my son's head as if he were a puppy.

Raina pinches the half-smoked cigarette between her thumb and index finger and extracts a puff. "Tom, any vices you care to indulge today?"

I shrug.

"Want a drag?"

I take the cigarette smoldering between my fingers and imagine inhaling deeply while everyone watches. It's been years since my last smoke. I drop the butt on the sidewalk and step on it.

"Sorry," I say. "I just don't think it's right in front of our son. Shall I start on dinner or is going out on Dad's dollar part of vice day?"

"We were thinking sushi," Raina says.

"And for the big guy?"

"Ben, what are you hungry for?" Raina asks.

"French fries," Ben says.

"Frank, would you care to join us?"

"Oh yeah," Raina says. "Actually, we already sprang for an extra ticket."

"Glad to have you, Frank."

* * *

RANDALL'S ISLAND. FROM AN encompassing ring of phosphorescent globes mounted on pillars, the surface of the yellow pavilion glows. A three-quarter moon hangs low over dimly lit Harlem across the river.

We're ushered through a smaller ante-tent where the lighting is low, eerie music hums, and the walls are draped with silk scarves and dresses, capes and top hats, glossy photo books, and wooden toys—a gift shop. Ben, perhaps not yet clued in that everything—soundtrack included—is for sale, doesn't plead for a souvenir, until, a few paces in, he spies a man spinning out egregiously large sticks of pink cotton candy. It's certain that more sugar today is not what he needs, but I don't resist. Cal and Frank's presence has me less inclined to play parent.

At our seats, I look up at the domed structure and recall my favorite scene in *Dumbo* when Casey Junior, the steam engine, takes the crew to a barren field outside some southern town. It's nighttime and it's pouring and suddenly all these faceless workers leap heroically from the train wielding sledgehammers and pick axes. Over the rhythm of their hammering and grunts they sing a song in low, sonorous voices, *We work all day, we work all night, we never learned to read or write*, and by the end of it, it's morning and we've seen the whole tent go up.

Three mute, red-nosed clowns come out and begin toying with the audience. One of them drops into a seat right behind us and musses my hair. Onto the stage strolls a tuxedoed man in a top hat. He chastises the clowns then welcomes us with a resounding delivery.

"Our show begins tonight," he says, "at the funeral of Jacques Dupont."

"What's a funeral?" Ben says.

"Shhh. It's a party held when someone dies—"

"Tom, it's not a party!"

"Why?"

"Shhh. It's when a group of friends get together to honor their friend."

"Cause why?"

"Because he's dead."

"Who's dead?"

"Jacques."

"Why?"

"Shhh. It's starting."

Portly Jacques, in tattered clothes, ambles on stage accompanied by two young women in white dresses, one blonde and one brunette. From the speakers, strings swell and then fall, evoking waves. Then Jacques is dragged away from the women, first backward, then from side to side. Then he's airborne. He struggles comically as wires attached to his lower back and shoulders propel him up and out over the audience. Ben joins the crowd in laughing at his misfortune. Eventually Jacques is allowed to rest on a rafter and watch as a band of eccentrically dressed clowns, including more than one little person and a bearded woman, march on stage playing an eerie waltz. A spotlight reveals a coffin at the top of the tent. Miraculously, the women in white are sitting elegantly on either end. A sleight of hand. The coffin and the women descend into a cloud of mist that has risen above the stage.

A fast electronic beat begins thumping and a bedroom scene rolls onstage, two oversized beds with smiling acrobats in children's pajamas bouncing and doing flips on the mattresses. The audience applauds and the show goes on.

* * *

AFTER THE SHOW, THE five of us are speeding down the FDR in Cal's vintage, diesel Mercedes. Ben is in a foul mood. *Dad, don't talk to Mom.* Then irrational. *Mom, I don't like other cars.* He's exhausted.

I'm in the front passenger seat. Raina sits in the back between Ben and Frank.

"Hey Ben," Frank says, "remember the tightrope walkers?"

He screams at Frank, though it's unclear what he's trying to say. Then he erupts in tears.

Raina is trying to calm him down.

"Oh, sweetie. It's okay. We'll be home soon and you can lie down. You must be very tired."

Ben is still wailing. He doesn't want to lie down. He's trying to reach under Raina's shirt. He hasn't breastfed in over a year. Then, with a wild look in his eye, Ben stops pouting. He sits up in his car seat, rears his head back, and vomits.

The projectile is shocking: all over the back of Cal's seat, even spraying Cal's neck, and dumping all over Raina's pants. Everyone is immediately consoling Ben, who's become strangely calm. We're on the FDR, somewhere in the fifties and it's decided that it doesn't make sense to pull over until we get to the gas station near our apartment.

We drive on for thirty or forty blocks with the wretched stench. Raina apologizes repeatedly to Cal. It's not unlikely that his car will never smell the same.

3

"Tom! Tom! Tom!"

Hands reach for my throat. I'm being suffocated. A scream wells up from deep within me. But the sound is muted. I'm in a vacuum. White waves through crimson air.

"TOM!!"

I lunge forward. I'm in the middle of the tiny floor space in our bedroom. Finally.

"Tom, are you alright?"

Raina is looking at me. Ben's looking at me too, standing up in his bed. They're both blurry.

"Don't worry, I'm not going to do it. She didn't get me."

There's a pause. I smile.

"Huh. I guess I'm not making sense," I say.

"No, you're not. But I'm glad you're okay. Christ, that was terrifying. You let out the worst screams I've ever heard. It was awful. It didn't sound anything like you."

Raina's shape sharpens—a frizz of snaky curls, face swollen from sleep. Her shoulders rise and fall. Then she whispers, "Tom, I thought there was someone in the house."

I turn to check on Ben. Cub-like, zipped into footed pajamas, his wide-eyed stillness suggests that he's witnessed something otherworldly. For a time, the three of us remain as we are, standing together in our bedroom. I listen to them breathe. I breathe too and feel calm.

I lift my son. His fuzzy arms and legs wrap around me. Raina wraps her arms around both of us. Then I place Ben back into his bed and draw up the blanket.

"I guess Daddy had a bad dream," I say. The clock by the window reads 3:48 A.M. "Let's all sleep in today."

My mind travels back inside the circus tent to the end of the first act, where Jacques is once again being swung side to side, the lights shifting from pink to yellow to deep red and fiery orange.

* * *

9:15. I WAKE IN a deserted room. The last time I slept this late it was a different decade.

I discover Ben, showered and dressed, seated cross-legged on the living room carpet, a few feet from the television. *Dora the Explorer*. A veteran of almost every episode, my son replies to Dora's questions efficiently and unemotionally, in a quiet, composed voice.

Raina is hunched over the kitchen sink scrubbing a frying pan.

"Good morning," I say. "How did you sleep?"

"Miserably," she says. "I've been up since four. I was way too shaken to fall back asleep. Tom, you scared the crap out of me last night."

"Sorry about that."

"I honestly thought someone was murdering you, or you were choking. You made these awful, high-pitched screams. I mean, are you alright? Do you remember the dream?"

"I'm not sure. Someone was trying to strangle me. But I'm alright now. I actually feel really good, refreshed." I note Raina's sullen expression and the dark circles under her eyes.

"Ben's already a half-hour late for school," she says. "I don't need to be at the office until one." She's being passive aggressive.

"How about I play hookie with Ben and let you sleep a few more hours?" I say.

Requiring no further encouragement, she sets down the pan, puts a hand on my arm and mutters, "I'm glad you're not dead," and retreats to the bedroom. She forgot to say goodbye to Ben.

I walk over and give him a kiss. "I'm going to take a quick shower and then I'll be ready to play. No school today."

"Okay, Daddy."

On my way into the bathroom, I pause in front of Raina's Olympus camera, slung, in its faded orange carrying case, over the back of a chair. It was probably her favorite possession for most of the years I've known her—the accomplice used to realize her most personal visions, her creative life. When Ben was born, she'd switched to digital to more easily distribute his picture among family and friends.

* * *

"I DON'T WANT TO go to the park!" Ben snaps and begins a mad crawl to the TV set, which accelerates into a dash in the direction of the bedroom, to his mom. I spring and clasp him from behind—hands fast on his hips. His legs and arms flail. He twists around and tries to scratch my face.

"Hey!" I say. "Listen to me. Your mom had a rough night. She needs sleep. Don't you dare wake her up." I stop and calm myself. I need a tactic. "Listen, I'm not taking you to school today. Now, Halloween's not for another three days, but do you want to wear your costume to the park?"

He doesn't look convinced.

"You don't want to be Superman?"

"Yeah! Daddy, I want to be Superman!"

I'm unlocking the front door, when my mind returns to the chair in the living room where Raina's camera hangs in its case. Ben is chomping at the bit now. I dart back inside and loop the camera over my neck. Up, up, and away.

* * *

BEN BOUNDS AHEAD. I jog close, chasing the red cape. Two different women put their hand to their mouth in a gesture of overcome emotion. A man exclaims, *It's a bird! It's a plane!*

On the subway platform, two twenty-something guys egg him on, *Dude, awesome*

Superman costume. You can totally fly. You have super strength. You can shoot lasers from your eyes. And you get the girl.

I know I was in school. High school, definitely. It must've been getting that invitation to my reunion a few weeks back that got me thinking about it. The date was for sometime near Christmas. Only in the dream, I wasn't even going to graduate. I had to learn something first to pass a course and be able to graduate. I was hopelessly behind, impossibly confused. I didn't know what it was I didn't know.

Then I'm in the boys' bathroom. But the walls recede forever. There are no stalls or urinals or sinks. Just tile. Those tiny one-inch by one-inch yellow-brown tiles. The floor is muddy. Black and watery with clumps of sludge. I move forward, barefoot. I'm completely naked. The door is locked. It's nighttime. I can peer out through a crack. I see the hallway and lockers.

When I turn back around a woman approaches from the infinite, tiled abyss. It's Jessie. Except it's not Jessie. It's Olga Petrova. Olga, who I've never seen and haven't thought about in weeks. Olga, yes, but physically, it's Jessie. It's Jessie's body, Jessie's face. Except something's different about the eyes, which are darker and somehow foreign to me. Her skin is white, almost fluorescent. Olga, you did it, I hear myself say. Olga/Jessie doesn't say anything, but she keeps walking closer. Closer still. And she's got this red flowing dress. It's transparent. And she takes a step closer. I'm terrified. And the dress slides off her shoulders and down her non-existent hips to the floor. She's now a man. But without genitals. No curves. She's totally emaciated. I can see straight into her white chest. One more step toward me. I'm up against the filthy wall. She puts her arms around me. Around my neck. She's a skeleton now. A corpse. I'm screaming. It's Raina. She's saying my name. *Tom! Tom! Tom!*

This is Bedford Avenue. This is a Rockaway Parkway–bound L Train. The next stop is...

BEN AND I PASS a Salvation Army, a hardware store, a pizzeria, a health food shop, an accessories boutique—each festively draped in fake spider webs and other Halloween decorations. With Ben's pace keeping steady, as opposed to his commonplace manic swing between clumsy dash and slumped over why-did-you-give-away-my-stroller slog, tranquility flows over me.

I'm relieved. To be with my son. Just the two of us, without Raina. It's been too long. But that's okay. Whatever has been is okay. No reason to think backward now. My mind is sailing to the future. There are a million places I want to show Ben. I'll take him to Astoria, to Wave Hill, to the Greenwood Cemetery, on the Staten Island Ferry, to Rockaway, to the Hudson Valley, and Sleepy Hollow. I'll teach him about the labor movement and about why it's important, even when you're down on individuals, to remain optimistic about mankind. And if he wants to know about something else, I'll teach him about that, too. If there's a question that I don't know an answer to, we'll look it up. Together.

Before Bedford leads us to the park there are two adjacent bars, each offering beer from the neighborhood's own Brooklyn Brewery. Ben skips ahead.

We enter McCarren Park and break into a steady jog across a barren baseball diamond. Futuristic stadium lights stand tall and alien-looking against the gray-blue sky, the way I imagine the wind-turbines that make the long shadows across the Nebraska prairie. Jessie.

We reach the playground where Ben tackles the slides. I take a seat on one of the benches, lay

Raina's camera gently next to me, and start in on the snacks I packed for us. A bagel and cream cheese. I have a sip of coffee. I take out my cell phone and call her.

"Hi. Tom..." Jessie says, "I'm really sorry. I'll be at the office soon. I'm just running a little late."

"You're not at the office? Oh, that's funny. Ben and I are in McCarren Park. I'm taking the day off. If you're still in Williamsburg, why don't you come join us?"

"Really? How funny." I think I hear the low rumblings of a male voice, though it could be the radio. "Are you sure that'd be okay?"

"Don't worry, I got your back."

Jessie laughs. "I can probably see you guys from my window. I'll be there in a few minutes, okay?"

A strikingly tall mother and her daughter enter through the playground gate. The mother is wearing some incredibly fashionable fur jacket and boots. She looks like a model. The blonde, curly-haired daughter sipping a juice box appears to be about Ben's age. The model unzips the girl's coat revealing a pink dress with purple and white lace. From her coat pocket, the model removes a plastic, jeweled tiara and places it on the girl's head. Another Halloween costume.

Ben runs toward the princess. The princess gives him a once over and goes back to her juice. Her mother excitedly taps the princess's shoulder and points out the S on Ben's chest, but the princess isn't having it. Ben races back to me and slaps my knee, grinning and pointing at the girl in the pink dress.

"She's a princess," I say.

He nods fervently and runs back over to the girl. This time, the princess has a change of heart. Then they're off running and giggling together. The princess leads the way up the twisty slide and Superman follows. The model and the labor lawyer take to their feet.

"Hi," I say. "I'm Tom."

"Kristina," she says.

"Your daughter seems very sweet."

"Thanks. Looks like they're getting along."

I look at Kristina again. *What would you do with all that leg?*

* * *

JESSIE, STRIDES THROUGH THE gate clutching a large white coffee cup. Her hair is wet, dark. I find myself bending and pressing my lips into her wrist, as if welcoming royalty.

"Tom. What're you doing?" She blushes.

"Sorry, I...I don't know. I guess I'm happy to see you."

I imagine she contemplates a kiss in return, but instead she gives my forearm a pinch. "Oh my god. Is that Ben? You've got to be kidding me. He is so adorable."

"Thanks." I'm grinning again.

"That costume is adorable. And that princess? Wow, they make such a cute couple. Halloween costumes?"

"Yup."

"He is such a charmer," Jessie says. "You guys trick-or-treating on Monday?"

"I think Frank's going to take him out."

"That's the babysitter, right?"

"Yup."

We settle into the steel benches. The princess lies down on her stomach at the top of the slide. Her dress, hiked to her thighs, exposes her purple tights, and she points emphatically to her backside, motioning for Ben, who's standing above her on the last rung of the ladder, to get on top of her. Ben hesitates. Then he gets on. The adults rise. The children ride down with Ben on top. The princess is delighted. They scale the ladder, and again, the princess sets to go.

"Rebecca," her mother calls timidly.

"Ben," I say.

The children scream their way down the slide. On the ground they rest, temporarily on top of each other, neither registering any sign of having heard their parent, and begin their ascent all over.

It's an awkward situation. Their game is totally innocent and sweet, of course, and amusing to watch. But as responsible, respectable parents, we're not permitted to stand idly by and allow this suggestive display to continue. Although, were it not for the the other two grown-ups present, I'd just as soon let it happen. I can't help wondering if Kristina feels the same.

When the children reach the top again, Ben lies down first, offering himself to the princess. And away they go, with Ben on bottom, grinning ear to ear. At least it's equal opportunity. This time I'm kneeling at the base of the slide. The princess starts climbing back up, but I hold onto Ben. I feel the women's gaze.

"Look," I say, "you don't have to stop playing. Just think of another game, okay?" He looks confused at first. But he's having such a good time. "Okay?"

"Okay, Daddy."

And to my surprise, that is that. The children continue to beam as they alter their sliding to a one-after-the-other train formation. And Kristina and I are relieved of blame. If, say in ten years time, our children turn out to be sexual deviants, it's not a result of our loose supervision at a Brooklyn playground.

Jessie and I each take sips of coffee and watch Ben trail the princess around the fenced-in park. Raina's camera case catches my eye.

"Oh yeah, I wanted to take some pictures," I say, pulling the camera out of its orange case. "I've never owned a real camera."

"You gotta take off the lens cap."

"All the greats," I say, examining the hardware, "like to envision their photograph in pure darkness. To see the image in their imagination."

"You're full of shit," she says.

"Perhaps," I say, leaping onto the bench, leaning back, and aiming wide for a panoramic shot.

I drag back the camera's lever with my thumb. The film, loaded and stretched, advances with a satisfying click, like cocking a shotgun. Something, I suppose, I've also never done.

"So whose camera is it?"

"Raina's."

"Oh."

I nudge Jessie's thigh with my foot. When she looks up, I snap her photo.

My phone vibrates in my pocket. I pull it out. Raina.

"Speak of the devil," I say—unwittingly, I immediately realize—and push the phone back into my pocket.

"Aren't you going to answer?"

"Artists at work can't be bothered," I say and snap her photo again. Then I jump down from the bench to take shots of my son.

Three photos down. I snap a low angle of Superman poised at the slide's summit to descend, an action shot of the princess and Superman sailing down together, hands raised ecstatically above their heads as if aboard a roller coaster. I turn the lens shaft counter-clockwise to 1/10. Suddenly I'm reminded of the movie *Blow Up*. I drop to my knees to get Ben heading down the slide. If I use up her film, I'll buy her some more.

Ben, for his part, behaves like a practiced subject. Arriving at a chain-link ladder, the princess pauses briefly, hands on her hips—a moment I capture with a click.

Jessie and Kristina may be asking themselves, costume or no costume, why I think it necessary to devote an entire roll of film to my son's prosaic morning at the park. Am I one of those parents who believe his child is that special? I do. I'm enjoying myself and have no intention of stopping.

My phone vibrates again, at which moment Ben, stepping off the playground's raised, rubbery surface to the concrete below, clambers onto one of the benches on the far end of the playground and lies on his belly. He's crawling on the bench, sliding along its smooth surface. When Ben reaches the end of one bench, he slides under the steel armrest, shoots up, turns, then drops down again, shimmying back under the armrest and along the bench in the other direction. The princess resumes her hands-on-hips pose, watching Ben's esoteric wiggles. I ponder putting an end to this perplexing game. It's weird, and probably pretty unclean. That costume may require dry-cleaning. But I let him be. The princess retreats to her mother for a snack, and I take a few backward paces to check in with my other companion.

Ben doubles back and completes another lap across the bench. Only this time, instead of standing and turning, he slides under the final armrest, and reaches out to the neighboring bench, cemented an arm's length away. He strains his arms and bucks his back, determined in his struggle, but he's too short, the gap too wide. But Ben thrusts himself forward. Bending at the waist, his torso flops and his head smacks down hard against the adjacent bench. Damn.

I slip out of the camera—Damn—I'm running—Damn, Damn—running to my son to dry his eyes, which, if they aren't watering yet, are surely about to flood.

I gather him in my arms and hoist him up, careful not to conk the other side of his head. The bench's edge has put a deep gash into his forehead. I can see layers of pink tissue and skin. Ben looks at me with confusion. A low whine stammers from his lips. His face contorts as blood issues from his wound. It streams into his eyes, into his mouth, over his chin, onto both our chests. My phone is vibrating.

"Call an ambulance," I cry. "Right now. Get an ambulance out here. Tell them to come to the northeast entrance of the Park." Ben's whine turns to shrieking sobs.

I tuck Ben in close and dash out the gate, flying over the grass, crossing the baseball diamond. Ben lets out tortured yells.

"It's okay. It's okay. Everything is gonna be alright," I say. "You're going to be okay. You're such a tough guy. We're gonna get you to the hospital. They're going to bandage you up and make you all better. Daddy's got you."

But what I'm thinking is—I've broken him.

The thought plays over and over again. I've broken him. I've broken him. I've broken my son. Oh god, what if there's brain damage? Ben, Ben, Ben. God I hope you heal. My beautiful son's got a hole in his head. He'll never be normal again. It's my fault. I let it happen.

"Mommy. I want Mommy."

"Mommy's coming, Ben. Mommy's coming."

The ambulance finally arrives and a boyish medic jumps out of the passenger side.

"I'm the boy's father," I say. "He hit his head pretty bad."

Jessie takes my hand in hers. I shake it free.

The medic sets about securing a large bandage over Ben's forehead—a hefty layer of gauze and two swatches of white tape.

"He can ride on your lap if he wants," says the medic.

The medic opens the trunk and motions me in. I climb up and he passes my son to me and then climbs in too. Jessie puts her foot on the bumper, about to get in.

"No," I say.

"I'll ride with you."

"I'm sorry."

"Tom, I want to make sure he's alright."

"In or out, ma'am? I need to close this door," says the medic.

"Out," I say. "You can't come."

"Hit the siren," the medic calls to his partner.

"I'm coming," Jessie says.

"Thanks for your help, Jessie, but please."

"You the boy's mother?"

"No, but I'm coming."

"Alright."

Jessie hops into the ambulance and the medic reaches to pull the doors closed behind her.

"Wait," I say and seize Jessie's wrist. "Listen to me. Get out of the ambulance. You can't come. I'll call you. Thanks for everything. Just please leave."

Jessie hesitates, gazing at me with plaintive eyes.

"Get the fuck out of the ambulance!"

Jessie turns away and jumps down. Doors are pulled and latched. Ben is crying.

"Thanks," I say.

The medic doesn't respond.

I see her through the window, receding.

My phone vibrates.

"Raina—"

"Why didn't you pick up your phone?! I've been trying to reach you all morning. Didn't you notice? I called you four times!"

"Raina, listen—"

"Do you have my camera, Tom?"

I reach for my neck where the camera strap had been. My hand traces the top of my son's silky head. I watch the fronts of the cars on the road through the rear window. It feels like I'm going backward.

"Tom?"

"No."

"No?"

"No. I mean, I had it. But... Raina listen to me—"

"Tom, I need it. I need my camera."

"For what?"

"What does it matter? I need it for work."

The medic avoids eye contact by looking forward, at the divider between us and the driver.

"Why didn't you pick up your phone when—"

"I'm sorry. Look, Raina—"

"I can't believe you—"

"—Wait. Raina, you have to listen to me. Raina... Raina, Ben hit his head. We're in an ambulance. Hello?"

The line is dead.

Ben is crying. "I want Mommy."

"Mommy's coming," I lie.

I call back. It just rings. I call again. The call goes straight to her voicemail. I picture the drama that's sure to ensue at the hospital when Raina doesn't show.

I try Raina again. It's ringing. Which hospital was it? I wish my son would stop crying.

Raina. Please answer my call.

November

1

My bruised and bandaged son sleeps perpendicular to my wife. Frank had reported concerned neighbors dropping generous fistfuls of candy into Ben's bag over Halloween, but that Ben had seemed to forget his disturbing appearance, as did his fellow nursery school trick-or-treaters. Frank said that a few times he felt as if some of the parents were looking at him with a certain suspicion as if he'd been responsible for Ben's injury. Yes, Raina had concurred, we've both gotten looks like that.

On the N train, while riding a car decked out with glossy posters of good-looking, starry-eyed youths enjoying Bud Light, it dawns on me that I've crossed into my twentieth year of riding the subway to work at Cunningham, Klein, and Levan. At the far end of the car, a neatly dressed, bespectacled man yells at an unwavering pitch about the return of our Lord.

42nd Street—the dreadlocked jazzmen are pounding and blowing out the same furious music in the same corridor underneath Lichtenstein's strange aquatic vessel. I deposit my bill and keep moving.

* * *

JESSIE AND I ARE making an uncharacteristic Tuesday afternoon trip to Dunkin' Donuts. Doreen's case is coming up, so I have her working extra days in order to properly prepare. She has her regular hazelnut coffee. I've decided to try something new: blueberry blend.

I'm inclined to begin by apologizing about the scene in the ambulance, though I'm unsure why I ought to be sorry. I haven't hurt anyone.

"So the arbitration is in thirteen days," I say.

Jessie nods.

"I'm going to build up and compile some of our questions about the clinic's termination procedure," I continue. "How soon was the complaint lodged? By whom? Who else heard the alleged conversation?"

Jessie nods again. We've discussed all this before.

I taste my fruity beverage. A letdown. I reach down for my notepad and realize I left my briefcase back at the office.

"Okay," I say. "So I've been thinking: while we can't know precisely what they'll pull out the day of the arbitration, I imagine there are two scenarios that could hurt us. One—they bring some indisputable piece of incriminating evidence such as a surveillance recording, something of that nature. But that's unlikely, not to mention unethical, because I've asked them to produce anything they've relied on in deciding to fire Doreen. Or two—a witness testimony from either a co-worker corroborating the complaint, or Olga herself. That's what I'm more concerned about. In all honesty, any witness they provide has the potential to come off sounding more credible and to appear altogether more stable than Doreen. Our letters, strong and impassioned as they are, may fall short when compared to living, breathing testimony, especially if Norcross doesn't credit what he might consider to be Doreen's self-serving denials. Arbitrators always scrutinize the testimony of the alleged wrongdoer."

"So what do we do, Tom?"

I hesitate a moment to appraise whether I'm being mocked, but Jessie's question is inflected with the appropriate level of concern.

"I propose," I say, "aside from using the letters, we try to corral a character witness. You know, a person of some repute to testify to the honorable nature of Doreen's ethic and standing."

"I know what a character witness is." She seems irritable. Maybe she's mad about the other day at the park.

"Well," I say. "What do you think?"

"Sounds right," Jessie says.

"The concern," I say, "is that we might overwhelm an arbitrator with too much character-related evidence. Certainly, an arbitrator like Norcross would have little tolerance for repetition. That's why we need just one stellar witness, assuming he or she exists. I thought a co-worker from the old clinic or maybe the supervisor, but then I thought, what about someone outside the healthcare field, someone with more universal respect. Unfortunately, I can't think of anyone like that who would also know Doreen.

"Maybe it won't work," I continue while Jessie sips thoughtfully. "Though it seemed like the right idea to me this morning. The director of the clinic in Queens could be good though, assuming Doreen's record there is as untarnished as she says. I don't know if she worked for any major volunteer groups back then. I doubt she knows any councilmen or politicians..."

"She mentioned that she went to church growing up, right? Maybe one of the clergymen?"

"A priest, that's perfect," I say. "I never would have thought of it."

"Where I grew up, the church leaders were some of the most respected members of the community."

* * *

RAINA SLEEPS COILED AWAY from me. Past her, just below, Ben snores.

Raina had made it to the hospital eventually. Although she was upset that she wasn't there during the stitching, the doctor, a confident, gentle man and a father of three who cleverly kept his office stocked with *Dora* episodes, had helped assuage her panic. Our son would be fine, he told us, just a matter of time for the body to heal itself. The scar on his forehead would grow lighter with each passing week.

The camera in its orange carrying case rests on the bureau. Jessie had retrieved it from the park playground and returned it to me when she came in on Monday.

I run my fingertips down Raina's leg, feeling the intermittent prick of tiny hairs. She's started shaving her legs again.

2

The lobby of the Sheraton is a sprawling, scrubbed and polished jungle. Waterfalls splash down into pools. There are potted, full-grown palm trees, and ceramic vases filled with wildflowers. Dreamy notes from a piano wander through the room.

Looking out from the glass elevator, Jessie and I spy Doreen near the revolving door. She's wearing the same green dress she wore to my office in October. She's having a conversation with a man. They appear to be arguing.

We wait for her on the couch in the small foyer, outside conference rooms 27A and 27B. When she arrives, she sits silently. She seems distracted.

An energetic young union rep approaches, offering firm handshakes for each of us. He's wearing his blue and yellow pin for Local 72.

"John McDougall," he says amicably. "Hi, Doreen. You ready to go? Attorney Claughlin is one of the best in the business, known throughout the land. He wins all of our cases."

"Thank you," Doreen says, "I feel so fortunate." Her eyes wander back toward the floor.

"Everything's all set for the Christmas party," McDougall says, flashing me a conspiratorial smile. "They say it's gonna be a big one. At the museum again this year. And I hear you're gonna be the man of the evening."

"One of them," I say. "This is Jessie Engel, a talented legal assistant at Cunningham, Klein, and Levan."

"Lovely to meet you," she says, shaking hands with McDougall.

Father Alexi arrives, overcoat over his arm, wearing his collar and spotless black attire. Doreen brightens when she sees him. Alexi has broad shoulders and a wide, serious face. The kind of guy who's always ready to dispense some profound, encouraging phrase or another.

In walks the opposition—three men in dark jackets. One of them wears a crisp pinstriped suit and bow-tie, hair parted and gelled. He surveys the room, does a double-take at the sight of the priest.

"Mr. Claughlin?" he asks.

"That's me," I say.

"Franklin Waxman, I'm representing the Coney Island Health Clinic. We were wondering if we might have a word with you in private."

"Before Norcross gets here?"

"I think we can clear up some things and save everyone some time."

I look around at my seated companions who look expectantly back at me.

"I suppose a little non-binding discussion is harmless," I say.

In the bare, windowless room, the six of us huddle around a long table. Waxman introduces his clients. The more muscular one is Kaplan, the physician-in-chief and executive director, and the heavy-set man is Sarnoff, an officer on the clinic's board of directors. Kaplan appears to be in his sixties, while Sarnoff doesn't look a day under ninety. Jessie, McDougall, and I sit on one side, the three of them on the other. They haven't brought along any witnesses. Waxman does the talking.

"I'd like to begin," he says, "by emphasizing that the foremost priority of the Coney Island Health Clinic is to give the highest quality of service to its patients and to the Coney Island community. My clients have always maintained a record of solid labor practices. They make a genuine effort to be considerate, judicious, and fair to all their workers."

His delivery sounds rehearsed.

"My clients are not in the practice of being called to arbitrate. We hope to avoid a protracted litigation, if you are willing—"

There's a knock at the door. Norcross's head pokes through the doorway.

"Good afternoon, gentlemen," he pauses when he spots Jessie, "and lady." He checks his watch theatrically. "The arbitration is set to begin in a minute. I know we all want to get started as quickly as possible. So, by all means take a few minutes. It's always better if the parties can reach a resolution, but if nothing seems to be developing, I'd like us to get on the record soon." He nods to me. "Hi, Tom. Waxman, right?"

"That's me," Waxman says. "Good to see you again."

"Likewise," Norcross says. "I'll check on you all in a few."

The door closes again.

"Let's cut to it," I say.

"Alright," Waxman says. "I'll let that be my segue. Our proposal is quite generous. In a show of goodwill, my clients are willing to let bygones be bygones and offer Ms. Grant reinstatement to her previous position."

"And what about her record?"

"We are also willing to offer her a clean slate by removing any misconduct from her permanent record."

Let bygones be bygones? What's the catch? Have I missed something?

Waxman continues, "My clients merely request recognition from Ms. Grant of what transpired in July."

"How would that work?"

"We ask that Ms. Grant sign a formal letter of apology pledging to respect the rules of patient confidentiality in future dealings with patients of the clinic."

Waxman reaches down into his briefcase and slides a single sheet of paper across the table.

"Alternatively, my clients are prepared to offer a clean record as well as eight weeks' back pay in exchange for her resignation and her agreement never to seek re-employment with the clinic."

The letter is exactly as he says, first the barest of apologies and then promising to do differently. The sentences are void of any specifics—no names, no dates, no context. As a contractual document, it's next to nothing; it promises to do only what she must in any event.

McDougal leans toward me and whispers, "What do you think?"

"I don't know. It seems good," I whisper back.

"It'd be great if we could get her back at that job." McDougal whispers. "A reinstatement would make the union look good. I think we'd come out looking strong."

"Right, I know," I whisper back. "As long as Doreen's happy with it, I think we'd better take it. But I'm going to try to get her more money."

"Can you do better on back pay?" I say to Waxman. "She's been out of work for four months."

"Let's be clear: Ms. Grant's termination was a unanimous decision."

"A unanimous decision?" I say. "An unjust termination is an unjust termination. Your client has yet to provide any evidence that Ms. Grant's termination was anything but. Unless you'd rather see what Norcross thinks, I suggest you come back with a better offer."

"Fine. There's no need to raise your voice, Mr. Claughlin," Waxman says. "How does two weeks sound?"

"Make it four."

Waxman glances at Sarnoff, then at Kaplan. He looks again at me and nods.

I rise. "If you'll excuse us while we confer with Ms. Grant."

Jessie, Doreen, McDougall, and I march into the neighboring conference room.

"Everything amicable in there? You guys making progress?" Norcross calls.

"Real progress," I say. "I just need to review matters with my side."

"Fantastic," says Norcross. "I'm delighted."

The four of us gather around the table. If I were in her position, I'd take the money and the scrubbed record and never set eyes on that place again. But the union's my client. I've got to look out for its interest. Doreen said she wanted her job back. Now, I've just got to get her to sign the letter.

"Okay, Doreen. They've given us an offer with two possible scenarios. In the first scenario you receive eight weeks of back pay and your record would be cleared, but you'd resign and wouldn't be able to work at the CIHC again. In the other scenario, you'd get your job back, your record is cleared, and you get a month paid. All you'd need to do is sign off on a statement acknowledging past misconduct and committing to adhere to the clinic's patient confidentiality rules."

"But I didn't do anything," Doreen says.

"While that may be the case, I don't think we're going to get a better offer than this. If we go forward, we run the risk of getting nothing— neither your job, nor the money. There are no guarantees in arbitration. I told you I'd do everything I could to get your job back. That's what you want, right?"

She looks down at the table where I've laid the letter.

"On the other hand, you could just take the back pay and walk."

"No." Doreen looks up at me. Her eyes are filled with tears. "I'll sign."

* * *

OUTSIDE THE SHERATON, THE nine of us congregate for one last round of handshakes. Each side holds a copy of the settlement. Kaplan tells Doreen he looks forward to having her back on the team.

Doreen thanks Kaplan, Sarnoff, and Waxman respectively. The two men from Coney Island trudge east toward the subway station. Norcross congratulates us, gives me a pat on the shoulder, and hails a cab. Father Alexi congratulates and embraces Doreen.

I nod to Waxman and pull him aside from the others.

"So what happened in there?"

Waxman smiles. "Things didn't quite materialize the way we hoped as far as evidence. Off the record? The firm has me focusing on another big fish right now. We've got a major anti-trust case coming up. Front page, above-the-fold type stuff. You understand." He puts a hand on my shoulder and winks.

Before departing, Father Alexi smiles broadly and says, "As Matthew tells us, He that endureth to the end shall be saved."

"Amen," Waxman says before turning and ducking into a town car.

"What a day for the union!" McDougal beams. "You were incredible in there, Claughlin. What did I tell you, Doreen? This guy's the best." He turns to Jessie. "I hope you were taking notes. You could learn from a guy like this. Hell, we all could." He claps his hand against my back. "I hope you all have excellent days. This one's worth celebrating!" He gives one more wave before heading uptown.

Doreen turns to me. "Thank you for everything you've done. Thank you."

"Maybe we'll cross paths again under different circumstances," I say. "At a union function, perhaps?"

"Yes," she says, "I'd like that."

"Me too," I say. "Good luck with everything."

Doreen takes off briskly down the sidewalk in the same direction as her employers. Jessie and I watch her until she disappears around the corner.

* * *

"Shall we have what Cunningham and I used to get?"

"What's that?"

"Pasta with clam sauce and gin and tonics."

"I like vodka," Jessie says. We're at the Italian restaurant in the Edison Hotel.

"The linguine alle vongole and two vodka tonics."

"Ah, very good," says the waiter, an older Italian man, "Very good. And for the pretty lady?"

"Just the drink," Jessie says. She's wearing a black v-neck dress. I was too preoccupied during the arbitration to notice. She's looking down at a compact mirror.

"I never do this," she says as she dabs herself in a circular motion with a soft brush. "Only for important events. I don't trust it to stay on right."

Her complexion is milky clean. It's like she's buffing marble.

"You look nice," I say.

The old waiter returns with our drinks. He smiles at Jessie.

"In Italy they would call you *donna bellissima*. That means *beautiful woman*. Are you going to the theatre tonight?"

"No, we're celebrating."

"Aha. Is she your daughter?"

"My partner, we're celebrating our first victory together."

"A victory? What did you win?"

"We won an honest woman her job back, plus back-pay for the time when she was out of work," Jessie says and gives the waiter a satisfied grin.

"Well, very good. Very good indeed. You must toast. In Italy we say *cento di questi giorni*. That means, *may you live for one hundred years*."

"And may all your victories be as smooth," I say to Jessie. We touch glasses and drink.

"She's going to make a great lawyer," I say. The waiter nods in approval before turning to attend to another table.

"So is she coming?" Jessie asks.

"Raina? She didn't pick up."

"I'm really happy we won. Doreen deserves what she got," Jessie says. "It's just that, with all that work we did. It's silly, I know. But I was looking forward to a struggle. I didn't want it to be easy. Is that crazy?"

"It's not crazy," I say. "I was ready for a fight too. But trust me, there'll be plenty of times in your career when you're going to wish cases would resolve like this one. Some lawyers never want to settle, but the good ones do, because they know they need to do what's best for their client. Ultimately you're not representing just one person. You're representing hundreds, or thousands or millions, depending on how you look at it. You always have the union's reputation on the line, not to mention the limitations of its resources." I shrug. "All things considered, this was a profitable day."

"You're right," Jessie says.

"Well, you are too," I say. "I don't know why they didn't just send us a letter two months ago. Would have saved them money. Would have saved us a lot of time and energy. It kills me knowing the union's money goes to enrich Norcross. But you're not sorry, are you?"

"No," she says, still looking down. She swirls the half-melted cubes in her glass.

"Sorry I got you involved, I mean."

"No."

"Good. I'm glad things worked out the way they did," I say. "It was nice to work with you. I mean, I'm glad to have shared it with someone."

"Do you think she really did it? Doreen—do you think she said all those nasty things?"

"It doesn't matter now," I say.

"Off the record?"

"I don't know."

"Do you mean it when you say I'm going to make a great lawyer?"

"I have no doubt."

"Thanks," Jessie says. She looks up at me. Water eyes. "Tell me how it was with you and Cunningham in the old days when you used to come here."

"I already told you about that," I say.

"Tell me again," she says. "Were you really the same age as me when you started at the firm?"

I think about Waxman and his talk of bigger fish. A guy like him could never understand.

The old waiter sets dinner between us.

"Buon appetitto," he says. "Another round?"

* * *

"THAT PERVERTED OLD WAITER called me beautiful." Jessie hiccups. "Twice!"

"What a character," I say.

We cross over 6th Avenue at 47th.

"He bought us all those drinks before the bartender even showed up."

"Creepy old man."

"I kinda liked him. Where should we go next?"

"To a bar," I say. "We'll walk this way until we find a good spot—though I'm afraid we'll hit the river before it happens."

"Do you know a place?"

A cold wind picks up behind us.

"It's good to win, isn't it?" I say.

"I suppose. It's all so new to me."

"Winning? Success? I doubt you're a stranger to that."

She stops and closes her eyes. "I feel good," she says. "It is a beautiful night, isn't it?"

"A beautiful night, yes, clear enough for stars," I say.

"You're really happy for her, aren't you? For Doreen."

"Yes."

"And you're happy for me?"

"Yes."

"I'm taking the bar soon, in January."

"Wow. So soon."

"Tom, are you happy?"

"Yes. I mean, I'm good. Are you happy?"

"I feel good."

We cross 5th Avenue.

"You know," Jessie says, "where I'm from, you could sit anywhere on a night like tonight and you'd be able to see so many more stars. I mean thousands more than you guys have ever seen. All those constellations you have stenciled up in Grand Central, you can actually see all of them. And thousands more. So many more, all perfectly clear. You can make up your own constellations..."

There's a vibration in my pocket. Raina.

"Hold that thought," I say. "Guess what?"

"What?" Raina answers.

"We did it."

"Did what?"

"We won her case."

"Whose case?"

"Doreen's. Doreen Grant. We won the case."

"Who's Doreen?"

"Who's Doreen? You know who she is. The receptionist...the healthcare worker...very sweet, good heart, a little bit odd."

"Wait, was she a receptionist or a healthcare worker?"

"A receptionist. At a health clinic. The one who helped everyone..."

"...Sorry..."

"What do you mean?"

"I must've forgotten."

I pivot away toward the wall of a building and speak more softly.

"Raina, I told you all about her."

"Look, Tom, I said I was—"

"I told you this morning I had an arbitration."

"Well, you know that's not a good time to tell me things when I'm getting ready."

"I can't believe this."

"I'm sorry, Tom. That's good that you won. I can't really talk—"

"Good? It's fucking great is what it is."

"Don't get so worked up. Have you been drinking?"

"No. Yes, I've had a drink. Hey, look, I'm sorry. I just got excited. I thought you knew this was a big day for me. I was hoping you could come meet me for a drink. We're celebrating. I wanted you to be there."

"Oh, Tom, I'm sorry. I didn't know. I made plans. But you go and have a nice night. Don't worry about coming home early. I can't really talk, I just wanted to—"

"Who's gonna put Ben to bed?"

"Frank will. Then I'll be home."

"I don't believe this."

"I'm proud of you, it's just that—"

"I know, you just can't talk right now."

"Tom..." Raina's voice is quiet.

"What?"

There's a pause.

"Good night," Raina says.

"You really don't remember?"

No answer.

"Raina...?"

The call has ended.

I feel a pat on my elbow. It's Jessie. Her dark hair catches in the wind.

"Is everything alright?" Her face glows against the night and the charge of speeding traffic. "Do you want me to go?"

"No. Don't leave," I say. "It's early. And I have a place for us to go. I've never taken anyone there. It's kind of a secret."

* * *

THE OVERHEAD FLUORESCENTS BUZZ in the after-dark silence. We duck past the empty guard desk, past the dormant elevators, which have been turned off for the night, and through the back door marked Exit. A hallway leads us through an unlocked door marked Employees Only; and then past storage rooms, a small office, bathrooms, a janitor's closet, and a freight elevator.

"In here," I say.

The odor is dank in the unlit compartment. I lift the door up manually, secure the latch, and feel for the top button. The elevator moans, lurches in place, and then begins a slow ascent.

Jessie giggles when I crack one of the beers. We'd grabbed a six-pack from a nearby bodega. I have a swig and hold out the can to her. She does the same, continuing to laugh between drinks. When the freight stops, I open the gate and take us down a hallway leading to a back stairway. We're at the fiftieth floor and have twelve more to go.

"I discovered this place years ago," I say as we climb. "Just wandered up without a second thought. It was kind of weird how simple it was. Everything unlocked and unguarded. It's funny being up there alone. I've thought about telling someone about it, but I wanted to make sure it was the right person, someone who'd understand. In the end, I figured if I wanted it to last, I ought to keep it to myself. It's really something, standing on top of the city. You're not going to believe it. It may not be Kansas, but..."

"Nebraska."

I wink and keep climbing.

At the final landing, I escort us, can of beer in one hand, briefcase in the other. There's a red box that I've never seen before rigged above the doorway. A camera, and the word STOP printed in red letters on the door handle are also new features. Above the handle is a new sign that reads, NO UNAUTHORIZED PERSONS ALLOWED. But we're well-meaning individuals. We work here.

I lean into the handle with my forearm. And the moment the door swings into the night, a shrill, deafening alarm bell blasts our unsuspecting ears. The sky disappears. The door slams.

"Fuck." I drop my beer. Suds pour out on my shoe.

"Tom?!"

I flee past Jessie, jerking her by the wrist, backward to the stairs.

"Let's go."

I'm tearing down steps, when her footsteps grow faint.

"Come on!" I call.

The alarm thunders, ricocheting around the walls.

"Tom, my shoes."

I double back and retrieve them where they've fallen.

We hit the fiftieth floor, fly out the narrow staircase and sprint down the hall. No time to risk the freight. Jessie's at my side. We dip into the main stairwell and this time Jessie flies ahead, descending now with agile grace. Leaping over steps, her black dress billows.

The alarm continues to blare.

"Forty more," I say.

"Thirty-nine," she calls.

I switch my briefcase to my outside hand and clasp the shoes with my fingers. At each bend, I swing myself, using my free hand, around the banister. Pushing off the railing, I sail over five and six steps at a time, thumping the floor at each landing, careening into walls. Jessie forges just ahead.

"Thirty more."

She laughs. Her feet rap the cement stairs faster and faster. Her laughs turn to shrieks, growing louder as her pace accelerates.

I yell, too.

A few flights farther down, she slips, tumbling for a step or two, before twisting around, and continuing to fall ass-backwards. She screams as she scrapes against four or five more steps before reaching up her hand and stopping herself just as her feet touch down on the next landing.

"You alright?" I call from a few flights up.

She straightens herself back out and gallops down the next flight.

Down and down, howling like banshees. Walls lose their corners and turn to liquid.

"Twenty more."

"Sixteen."

"Fifteen."

"Eleven."

Two floors below I spot Ricky, the night watchman, lumbering up toward us. I watch Jessie fly past him. Ricky halts, perplexed, and begins to turn when I bulldoze by. Then we're out, across the lobby, back into the street.

Jessie takes a few bare tights-against-concrete strides and stops, hands on her hips, chest heaving.

"Oh my god. I'm so fucking dizzy," she says.

I scoop her up and carry her to the corner.

"South," I direct, when we're safely inside a cab.

"Okay," says the cabbie, eyeing my beautiful, slumped-over companion and me in the rearview, "but I'll need more than that."

"Let's start by getting us out of here."

"Okay, boss, meter's running."

The cabbie deftly slides the car across two lanes and then swings it right out into the busiest intersection in Manhattan. The line of cars waiting to take a left hold down their horns, but the sound quiets, as the cabbie guns it through the intersection—ahead of the uptown rush—and down 41st Street.

"Name is Omar," he says. "You got the best driver in the five boroughs. I'm old-school."

"Good to hear," I say, still regaining my breath. "Me too."

"I gotta ask," Omar says. "Am I complicit in some kind of crime?"

"Not really," I say. "Strictly white-collar stuff."

"Cool," says Omar. "You guys always got the best lawyers."

"We are lawyers," Jessie says laughing.

"Even better."

Jessie has wrapped her arm in mine. She lifts up one of her legs over my lap and inspects the raw skin on her knee. Her tights are torn. Blood oozes over the white surface, disappearing under the fabric. She leaves the leg there. I bend down and slip her shoes back on her feet.

She whispers into my ear. "Let's go home." Her whisper is gentle. "Can we go home, Tom?"

Her lips touch my cheek.

"To Williamsburg," I say to Omar. "You know how to go?"

"I know how to get everywhere," Omar says.

In a moment we've reached the FDR, Omar winds us right, and soon we're picking up speed, riding the island's edge to the bridge.

* * *

WE KISS AS WE free ourselves from our overcoats. She shuts the door and turns the dead bolt. We kiss and my hands slide down her sides to her waist.

"Let's have some water," she says.

"Good idea," I say.

But then I drop to my knees atop our fallen coats—blocking her path—and duck beneath her dress, where I inch down her tights, kissing each new band of uncovered skin. I pull off each of her shoes. With two hands I grab her tights and rip them apart at the crotch, then bring them down to her ankles. Her thighs are stocks of alabaster white. I kiss them all the way up. Her black underwear is warm and wet. I remove that too and glide my tongue between her legs, up the thin strip of hair, and along her abdomen to her navel. Then I part her lips with my hand. Jessie's thighs clamp against my ears. The distant, hollow sound of an ear to a conch shell.

3

Doreen in her green dress, head bowed, sits precisely as she'd been on one side of the wooden table in the windowless conference room on the twenty-seventh floor of the Sheraton Hotel. She's flanked by Jessie and McDougall. The clinic's letter lies before her. Her employers and their lawyer sit across from her and wait. We're all witnesses, waiting and watching expectantly. Doreen takes the pen, puts it to paper, and signs. Then she raises her head and stares at me. And I see that there's blood streaming down from a gash in her forehead.

I sit up in my bed and touch my hand to my brow. It's damp with sweat. I roll over and reach out to put an arm around Raina. It's Jessie.

My overcoat and briefcase are by the door. I slide out of her bed and gather my clothes.

* * *

WILLIAMSBURG. THE SUN IS just beginning to peer pensively through the treetops. As I walk along the eastern border of McCarren Park, I contemplate a quick pass by the scene of Ben's accident. No, I'll revisit the grounds with Ben when he's older. *Look here, Ben. See this bench? You were only three and a half and I was supposed to be watching you. I was watching you. I watched you while you tried to crawl from one bench to another without touching the ground and fell right through. I thought your mom was never going to speak to me again. But she did. I was so terrified when I peeled you off the ground. You have no idea. But those doctors did a great job. Sewed you up good as new. Just the faintest scar now, huh? You can barely even notice it. The point is, things work out. You can be anything you want to be. Just between you and me, when it comes to your own life, things work out. When it seems everything is falling apart, like the world is splitting, sometimes you just need to get some more sleep and look at things fresh in the morning. Or better yet, to dig harder into your work. At least that's what I've always done.*

* * *

I TURN THE KEY gently in the lock. A figure sleeps on the sofa. It's Frank. His shoes are lined up neatly at one end. Next to his shoes is a paperback atop a folded sweater. I step closer. Frank moves faintly and then is still. If he's faking or half-faking sleep, I don't blame him for not wanting to converse at this early hour. He may not yet feel ready to explain why he's sleeping in my apartment.

I tip-toe past my son and slip into bed beside Raina, who sleeps where I usually do, facing the window.

"Have you been here a while?" She murmurs without turning. Her half-conscious voice is soft and lilting.

"A little while."

"Did you have a nice night?"

"Uh huh."

"Frank's building was being sprayed for bugs so I said he could stay here. Is that okay?"

"Of course."

"Okay," she says and reaches a limp hand back that doesn't quite make it to me. Her heavy breathing resumes. She has no idea. She'll go back to work tomorrow. So will I.

So will Jessie. And so will Doreen. I take Raina's hand, give it a light squeeze and set it back by her side.

December

1

"You get in trouble and I'll save you," Ben says, wielding a plastic Superman figure.

I hold a plastic Dora the Explorer figure.

"How about you think of this next one?" I say.

Raina kissed us each goodbye some time ago, and Ben and I have been playing for the last hour.

"No, you," my son says. His arms flap with agitation.

"How about we do one more mission?"

"Okay, go!"

He scampers across the room, crouches behind the armchair, and cries, "Call me when you need me."

Ben hops up and down behind the chair, eager to execute another mission. We call each rescue a mission. There is no fluidity to our game, just a series of missions—a hairy situation for Dora and a near instantaneous fly-in rescue from Superman. My son has no use for any kind of foreplay, no need for suspense or context, so missions are completed as quickly as I can think them up. My job is to keep getting Dora in trouble. So far I have had Dora attacked by all kinds of prey, suffer every type of natural disaster, need food, need medicine, lose track of her friend, lose track of her parents, get nearly crushed by train and truck, and even just get scared and want a hug. Superman has been there for her every time.

"Do you know what one more means?" I ask him, holding up my index finger.

"Yes," he nods. "C'mon, just do it, Daddy." He retreats lower behind his alcove to watch for my signal.

"Alright, then. I'm just going to climb up this mountain." I say in my Dora voice, walking the figure up to the top of the couch. "Uh-oh, it's pretty windy up here. Oh no, here comes a giant gust!"

I puff my cheeks out and then blow on Dora. Ben starts giggling. I do it again, bigger. Then again. It's hard to resist such an appreciative audience. I swell my cheeks until I'm laughing too. One more prodigious draft, and— "Help! Superman! Help! I'm faaaaaaalliiiing!"

Ben charges across the room, hurrying toward the back of the couch where I'm lowering Dora downward in slow motion. Superman's outstretched arms catch her just before she hits the floor.

"Thank you for saving me, Superman."

"You're welcome, Dora," Ben says, and in the same breath, "Daddy, let's do one more."

"Time to clean up," I say.

"But I don't want to clean up." Tears are already there.

"It's okay." I say. "No reason to be sad. More Dora and Superman later, they need to rest. Let's look at the movie page." I place Dora in the toy bucket, but Ben holds onto Superman. "Do you need to rest?"

"No," he whines. "What's the movie page?"

I pluck the Arts section of the *Times* off the table and take a seat on the couch. "Come look," I say.

Ben climbs into my lap. A four-piece rock band poses on the front page. I've never heard of them before. "Musicians," I say. "There's a keyboardist, and a drummer, and a guitar player, and another guitar player, or I guess a bass player."

"I like guitar," Ben says pointing to the front man. "I want to play guitar." He does a strumming motion on his belly.

"Pretty good. Maybe you'll be a guitar player someday."

I flip the paper over to find the Index.

"I like that," Ben says. He points his finger at a close-up photograph of four smiling Rockettes in the kick line, performing their Christmas spectacular. The women clad in sequined leotards and Statue-of-Liberty tiaras are captured at the height of one of their magnificently high kicks. "I like that, Daddy."

"Good," I say. "Those are dancers." It says they do over 1,500 kicks a day. I steal a sideways peek at my son: upturned nose, long eyelashes, silky brown hair, dressed in a spotless, newly laundered, blue and green striped polo shirt and tan corduroys. He beams, momentarily intoxicated, at the sight of long, smooth legs. Superheroes, guitars, and girls.

* * *

HAND IN HAND, WE enter the movie theatre at Lincoln Center to see a 10:45 A.M. showing of *The Polar Express*. I've never been in a movie theatre this early.

"Take the escalator to the fourth floor," says the woman behind the box-office window.

"Escabata!" Ben screams.

The young woman puts her hand to her mouth and laughs.

"You heard that, Ben? Three of 'em." I say.

"I love escabatas."

"You have an adorable son," she says.

I lift Ben, who's still clutching Superman, onto the counter to give the woman a better look.

* * *

WE TAKE SEATS BEHIND a well-dressed, platinum blond mother of three. Her two boys and girl are dressed in identical red sweaters. Triplets maybe. The previews begin, and I listen to the triplets gripe with one another while circulating two bags of gummy, sugary snacks among themselves.

During the opening credits, I demonstrate how to put on the 3D glasses the usher handed us on our way in. Ben shakes his head.

"I don't want to wear those," he protests.

I motion for him to whisper.

"It's okay," I say, soothingly as I can. "It's not scary. It just makes the movie look different."

He's not having it. I look around at the other kids wearing their glasses.

On screen, the nameless young boy, unable to sleep on Christmas Eve, is delivering a monologue in which he doubts Santa's existence by reviewing certain facts: no one lives in the North Pole. And even if someone did, one person couldn't possibly deliver all those presents unless they were traveling at light speed.

"But Ben," I say, "it will help you see the movie."

Ben reaches for my face to pull off my glasses. "I don't want you to wear them, Daddy."

"Alright," I concede, "I won't wear them."

Without the glasses the picture stays clear for certain stagnant moments but shortly goes maddeningly fuzzy every time there's movement. When The Polar Express comes roaring through the back yard, rattling the entire house, everything—the boy's hair, the bed-sheets, the curtains, the walls—all double, then triple and quadruple in successive blurry layers. It's like being extremely drunk. Only not as fun.

Ben stares bravely forward at the screen, dipping his hand into our bag of popcorn like the seasoned movie-goer he's fast becoming. The movie boy gets on the train and finds a golden ticket in his pajamas. The conductor provides hot chocolate. The children sing a song. I slip on the glasses. The steam rising from the mugs has impressive depth.

However long the moviemakers want to draw out the original scenes, something different is going to have to happen to fill out a full-length movie. And then it does, when the boy, in a gesture of kindness, sets out to return a young girl's ticket but drops it when crossing cars. The ticket takes an astonishing journey through the woods, under hoofs, inside beaks, and back, as a perilous chase ensues between boy and ticket atop the train's roof. The sound of the wind and the chugging wheels moves from side to side to side to side as if the train were traveling in a circle around the theatre. Mid-chase, a crazed hobo appears.

"I'm the king of the North Pole," the hobo says.

"Isn't Santa the king?" the boy asks.

"Do you believe in Santa?"

"I want to but I don't want to be tricked."

"Seeing is believing."

"Do you believe in ghosts?" asks the hobo.

"No," says the boy.

"Interesting," says the hobo and disappears.

The triplets in front of us get restless. "Where's Santa?" they beseech their mom. This sentiment continues to grow through the theatre. Other kids ask their accompanying adults.

I take off my glasses and look at Ben who stares intently upon the unfocused screen. There's almost no chance he's following the film. I'm surprised it doesn't make him nauseous.

I kiss him on the cheek and whisper, "Do you like the movie?"

He shrugs.

"Do you want to try the glasses?"

He shakes his head.

"Do you understand what's happening?"

"Where's Santa?" he asks.

"He's coming," I say. "They haven't reached the North Pole yet."

"Cause why?"

"It takes a long time."

The movie boy and the girl sing a ballad in the caboose. The song is about faith. The actors on screen appear neither real nor animated.

They're something in-between. As the duet crescendos, the northern lights emerge in spectacular fashion. From the audience, a young voice calls, "Where's Rudolph?" Another high-pitched voice asks, "Where's Frosty?"

"Shhh," says the nanny.

And all of a sudden, I can't take it any longer. I start to laugh. It's that spontaneous, uncontrollable laughter. I'm on the verge of a rare fit of hysterics.

"Daddy, what's funny?"

I'm sitting in a giant hi-tech theatre with eight pre-kindergarteners at eleven in the morning.

"C'mon, Daddy, what's funny?"

Ben looks adorable. I signal for him to hold his thought while I attempt to catch my breath.

But then, incited by the example of the first curious and impatient child, the other children follow suit. There's a host of *Where's Santa?*'s. Then again the same child asks, *Where's Rudolph? Where's Frosty?* Each question is answered with a barrage of shushes. *Where's the Grinch? Where's Elmo?* they want to know. The triplets lead the charge. Like me, fighting harder now to stifle my amusement, they're really beginning to enjoy themselves. Their mother isn't.

"Where's Mrs. Claus?" one of the boy triplets shouts.

"Where are my underpants?" says his brother.

All the children erupt with laughter. Anarchy is triumphing. In an attempt to smother the revolution, the triplets' mother unleashes a volley of fiercely whispered threats. I can see that Ben is very stimulated by this disruption and his father's laughter.

To my surprise, Ben lets one fly.

"Where are my underpants?" he says, copying the intonation of the older boy.

I laugh even harder. I can't stop myself now, my son is so endearing. Luckily, the chuckles of the children largely muffle my own, but Ben still hears me. He looks at me, somewhat puzzled, for he's still not exactly sure what is so funny. Nor am I really. But then, as if understanding something, if only that a good time is to be had, Ben flashes a sly and cheerful smile and begins to laugh along with me. He stands up on his seat, leans over, and whispers into my ear, "underpants."

His eyes are wet with tears. Mine are too. We're both shocked at the sight of the enraged mother when she whips around in her seat looking like an extraterrestrial in her 3D glasses. She says sharply to me, "Can you please control your child?!"

I manage a nod.

I turn to Ben and ask him, "Do you want to go?"

"Okay!" he says.

As we shuffle to the exit, I look up and watch the movie boy being lectured by the conductor, whose voice and message is the same as the hobo. "Seeing is believing," the conductor says. The triplets are throwing candy at one another. "Sometimes," the conductor says, "The most real things in the world are the things you can't see."

Ben wears a big grin when he ambles up to the one kids' urinal in the movie theatre's bathroom. I help him to unbutton his corduroys and pull down his underwear. As he pees, he continues to grin.

"That was a funny movie, Daddy."

* * *

SURFACING, SON IN TOW, from the Union Square station. I direct us north, compelled to extend our morning's outing and delay our inevitable return. For most of December's daylight hours, skateboarding and radical politics give way to Christmas shopping.

At the pet shop, automated snowmen made of Christmas lights sweep brooms and wave at intervals. We pass a sushi restaurant with a running waterfall splashing down in the entryway and an electronics shop displaying miniature models of old cars. When a customer exits, a tinny, robotic rendition of "Deck the Halls" leaks out. We pass an organic soap and bodywash shop with a large cutout of a wholesome model who, with gift in lap, looks up gratefully at her unpictured benefactor. We pass a sporting goods shop with mannequin-skiers and snowboarders—knees bent in their respective mid-slope poses—clad in sleek, futuristic outerwear and dark glasses as well as Christmas wreaths. We stop and look in on a storefront, set back from the street, situated behind fluted columns, where red and pink candles held by a crystal chandelier glow against a reflective backdrop of silver linens and jagged stalactites, below which, an upright bear wearing ice skates makes a continuous figure eight.

A posh-looking home-furniture store exhibits a green marble tub with brass faucets, a stainless-steel oven with six gas-top burners, and a granite countertop below mounted cherrywood cabinets. It strikes me as the type of store I've never bothered to see the inside of, but would like now to peruse.

"We can look," I say to Ben as we step up to the entrance, "but you have to hold my hand."

To the right of the door a quote in spare white lettering reads: "The details are not details. They make the product."

The door swings open with the sound of wind chimes and reveals a vast rectangular floor divided into a maze of numerous, interlocking rooms or, more precisely, displays of rooms. Nothing by way of four conjoined walls literally divides one room from the next but the borders are clear because each space is uniquely furnished and thus self-contained. Together we navigate, crossing first through a dining room with a long table stained to a deep finish set sparsely for four, and then through another such room with a curved table of purple glass set for two with champagne glasses. Next to the table is a hulking, abstract metallic sculpture. Stenciled onto one of the floor's many columns: "An interesting plainness is the most difficult and precious thing to achieve."

At various locations between rooms there are small wooden desks where either a pleasant-looking, chicly dressed young man or woman sits before a laptop. As we step past one desk into a plush living room, one of the young men asks, without getting up, if he can help. "That's okay," I say, taking one of his business cards to be polite, "just trying to get a feel for what I might like."

"Ah," the man says, "well, please, feel free to linger. Take your time. Let me know if you have any questions."

Ben and I take a seat on a large asymmetrical burgundy sofa. It's very comfortable.

"How does it feel?" I ask Ben.

Ben has become quiet and introspective. Maybe it's the pastoral music carrying serenely from the speakers on the ceiling. He rubs the ribbed fabric between his fingers. "I like it, Daddy."

"Me too," I say and flip up the plastic price tag hanging from the couch's arm. It's a cool five grand. Expensive, I think, but nice. It's hard to set a price on something you look at and use every day. The right addition could change everything.

From a long-necked lamp arched half-way over the sofa, a convex bulb leans gracefully downward, emitting a mellow glow. I rotate a silver knob at the lamp's base. The warm light sensitively dims and brightens to my subtlest twist.

"I want to try," Ben says.

Before sliding over I glance at the price tag. Two grand.

Ben and I continue strolling the rooms as if touring an estate. Every object, even those bearing the solidity and refinement of something older, radiates newness. The mystery inherently lurking in the sheen of a mahogany bedpost is not for what has been but rather for what might be. We pass a column that reads: "The urge for good design is the same as the urge to go on living." And another: "What you make is important."

A coffee table topped with glossy-leafed photo books of Midwestern barns and the Dalai Lama's travels, and a writer's desk with a copy of *Strunk & White* and a slim volume of e.e. cummings make it nearly impossible to simply stop at imagining a new home without going just a bit further and inventing a new life.

I'm sure we'll be living on the Upper West Side soon. We can afford it, especially now that Raina's back to work. We'll have two or three bedrooms. Maybe a study for Raina. Things will be better then. We'll be one of those couples. We'll send Ben to a private school. Drink lattes. Shop at Zabar's. I'll join a gym. Maybe Raina will take up yoga again. We'll make friends with other parents. Maybe even have another kid. Raina always used to talk about having two.

"Daddy, what's up there?" Ben points excitedly to a spiral staircase.

The upstairs is entirely devoted to bedrooms featuring sumptuous, white-mattressed beds of every size. Ben and I go straight for the kings and queens, their soft down comforters stretching erotically wide. Without fanfare, the first king we come to, draped in a soothing sea-foam green throw and plain white pillowcases, diminishes the memory of Raina's and my paltry full. We hop on, sense the security of powerfully wound springs under fluffy covers. At present there are no sales people up here. I feign a deep sleep before shooting up with a start. Ben laughs. I tickle him under his chin and behind his knees. I lie on my back and hoist him up on my feet. Superman.

* * *

BACK HOME. I KNEEL over and tuck Ben's sheets up to his neck, lean a sippy-cup of water against the wooden guard so he can reach it when he wakes, and kiss him.

"I love you, Daddy."

"I thought you were asleep."

"Almost."

"I had a really great morning with you."

"Me too."

"Okay, now go to sleep."

"Okay. But, Daddy?"

"Yes?"

"Are you gonna be there when I wake up?"

"Yes, of course."

"I love you, Daddy."

"I love you too."

When I leave the bedroom, Raina is facing me. She's come home undetected while I was reading *Pinocchio*, and stands now, at the other side of the living room, leaning expectantly back against the table.

"I've been listening," my wife says softly. She steps toward me.

"To what?"

"To what a great father you are. He's lucky. And so am I."

My wife and I meet in the middle of the room where she leans in for a kiss.

"But you're a lousy photographer," she says, motioning behind her.

I swallow hard. The photos. I picture Jessie posing for me in the viewfinder that morning at the park—hair wet, cheeks red, smiling drolly, seductively—then her unclothed body, writhing rabid in her bed. There they are: a small pile, four by six, stacked on the living room table.

2

Friday. Raina's late. The union Christmas party—to which the office of Cunningham, Klein, and Levan is invited every year—had been rescheduled from Tuesday on account of the transit strike, which officially ended yesterday afternoon. We'd planned on leaving as soon as Frank arrived. Frank was supposed to be here twenty minutes ago.

Dumbo is in the midst of blowing his first shot at stardom by tripping on his ears, the blunder that will demote him to the role of clown and freak. Ben giggles over the routine gone wrong. I dig out the Johnny Walker. I've opted for a black suit and tie.

A key turns in the lock. At the first glimmer of Frank's emergent figure, Ben leaps from the table and wraps his arms around Frank's skinny thighs, tugging at the hem of his jacket. Ben is fully ready to begin whatever game the two have been playing as of late. When he spots me sitting on the couch, his face sours.

"You go away, Daddy," he commands.

"That's not very nice," Frank says.

"Listen," I say to Ben. "This is my house too. Now, I'm going to leave as soon as Mom gets home, but if you want, I can go into the bedroom while you two play out here."

Just as Ben considers this, a clunky cadenza of horns projects from the miniature DVD player that's been left running on the table. The music signals the entrance of the dancing pink elephants, the stars of Dumbo's madcap hallucination. Over an infectious big-band march, an unseen choir eerily chants, "Hey look! Hey look! Pink elephants on parade!"

"Ooh! I want to watch this part," Ben says and dashes back to the table. Frank takes a seat next to him, and I'm not asked to leave. Ben is, as always, transfixed by the psychedelic sequence.

"How're things?" I ask.

"Good," Frank says. "Thanks."

"Making any art these days?"

"Not exactly."

"New designs?"

"Actually, I've been writing."

"Oh. I didn't know you did that. Are you working for anyone?"

"No, nothing like that," Franks says. "Just, you know, for myself."

"Fiction? Nonfiction?"

"Fiction."

"Fiction, wow, that's great. Maybe you can become a famous novelist and hang out with Ben forever."

"I suppose you already know this," I say, "but Ben talks about you all the time. He's so attached to you."

Frank smiles and glances down at his feet. He's embarrassed.

"That's sweet," he says.

"If you ever leave us, you'll have to join witness protection."

The lock turns again. It's Raina. Ben gives her a similarly ecstatic greeting. My wife smothers his cheeks with kisses and says hi to Frank. "Sorry I'm late, I'll just be a few minutes." Unloading her coat and bag on the recliner, she disappears into the bathroom.

I find her topless and bent over, pulling down her stockings.

"What're you doing?" I say.

She turns, startled, fully naked.

"You scared me."

"Sorry," I say. "Why are you getting undressed?"

She surveys herself in the mirror. Freshly trimmed under the bathroom light.

"I want to take a quick shower—"

I plant a kiss on her mouth and cup her breast with one hand.

"We're already late," I say placing my other hand between her legs. She's warm.

"No," she says. "Tom, not now. I don't want to make us any later."

She pivots away and steps into the tub. I sit on the toilet and watch her silhouette through the curtain.

"Sorry to be doing this," she says over the shower. "I was just feeling gross. We'll take a taxi. I'm going to wear heels so a car will be nice for me. We're not too late, are we?" She spreads her legs and soaps between them.

"We're not too late," I say.

"What?"

I say it louder.

"Good. I know you're excited to see your lovely assistant, although I guess you get to see her every day."

"Who, Jessie?" I say.

"How many do you have? The one from Kansas."

"She's from Nebraska."

"Well, she's beautiful."

"Funny you should mention her," I say. "I actually haven't seen her in a while. She took a couple weeks off to visit her folks. She's getting ready for the bar. Tonight will be the first time I've seen her since she left."

Raina cuts the shower, steps out and begins toweling off. "What?" she says. "Sorry, I couldn't hear you."

"Never mind. Get some clothes on."

Raina goes to the sink and applies mascara. I kiss her on the cheek and head for the door. In the middle of the living room carpet, Ben sits cross-legged and alone. His eyes are tightly shut and he counts out loud. Dumbo's saga has been paused just shy of resolution. I enter the kitchen where the lights are off, draw the sliding door and retrieve the Johnny Walker from the cabinet.

"Mr. Claughlin?"

"Is that you, Frank?" He's tucked in a corner.

"Yeah. We're playing hide-and-go-seek."

I have another pull, and return the bottle to the cabinet. "I'll try not to give you away," I say. "Raina, I'm going to wait outside," I call.

"Say good night to Ben," she shouts back from the bathroom. Ben is in the bedroom lifting the covers off our mattress.

"Do you want to come give your dad a hug and a kiss good night?"

"No, Daddy. I have to find Frank."

"Come on, Ben. Give me a hug and a kiss."

"No, Daddy! Go away."

"Okay then, see you tomorrow. I love you."

I call again to Raina. "I'll be out front."

* * *

"I WISH YOU WOULDN'T do that," Raina says.

"Do what?" I say. I'm looking out the window at New Jersey. We've been silent most of the cab ride.

"Leave without saying good night to your son."

"I did say good night."

"I mean a proper good night. With a hug and kiss. He's only three years old, Tom, he needs that."

"He was busy having a good time with Frank. I didn't want to interrupt. Plus, he wouldn't let me, anyway."

She looks out the window on her side.

"What?" I say.

"Nothing," she says. "I just think you're being childish."

"I'm being childish, you're being..." I trail off. "Well, maybe if you didn't..."

"Didn't what?"

"Nothing," I say. I try letting more blocks pass. "This is bullshit," I mutter under my breath. My mouth just kind of does it.

"What did you just say?"

"Nothing," I say. "Really, Raina, nothing."

"What's gotten into you?"

"Nothing."

"I'm fine," I say. "I'm happy. Look, we're almost there."

"Tom?"

"What?"

"You're not going to start..."

"What?"

"Nothing," she says. "I'm happy too."

The cab pulls up to the Folk Art Museum on 53rd.

"Tomorrow would've been my dad's birthday."

"I know," she says.

"I'm being honored tonight," I say.

She gives my hand a squeeze. "I know," she says. "He would've been proud of you."

I lean in and kiss her on the cheek. The driver hands me my receipt.

* * *

THE ROOM IS PACKED and dark. Faces and limbs glow copper under the lights. Christmas music politely swings.

A few paces in, I'm greeted by Margie Susman, an energetic, salt-and-pepper-haired director of education, and her husband, Mike. It's clear Raina has forgotten their names and they hers. I introduce everyone.

I imagine drinks are to be found somewhere in the back. Before I manage to lead us there we run into John McKibbins, the Teamster Local's president, and his wife, Carolyn, and then into Lamar Jackson, business agent for the United Industrial Workers Local and his wife, Cecile. We say a brief hello to my firm's senior partner, Henry Klein, who's more focused on steadying his twitching hand in order to dip a celery rod into the hill of sour cream on his plate, and to his wife, Sarah. And we say hi to Margaret, who informs us that her date has taken sick—a disappointment for all concerned. Then there's Harold Meyer, union rep for the Sheet Metal Workers and his wife, Catherine, and then Stanley O'Connor, vice president of the Amalgamated Bus Drivers' Union and his wife, Yuka. There's a lot of speculation as to how the transit workers' strike will resolve. Bus and subway services have resumed for now. I steal another glass of red off the tray of a passing waiter.

"You doing alright?" I ask Raina.

"I'm fine," she says. "You know how I get at these things." We've finally made it to the drink line.

"You seem bored," I say.

"Come on..." she starts, but then pauses and stares up past my shoulder. "Behind you, it's Kansas."

There she is. Jessie, alone in the stairwell, wielding a vodka tonic, advancing leisurely down the steps in a long white dress, red cardigan, green heels, hair up, lipstick on. She's the vision of menacing youth, unable to know the effect of her electrifying descent on our middle-aged party. She spies my wife and me standing below her. She waves.

"Hey you," Jessie says, slipping into line next to us.

"You're back," I say.

"Yeah. It was a great trip. I hadn't been home in over a year. I could tell my family was starting to wonder."

I'm grinning.

"The date of the bar is getting close. I'm so anxious."

"If A intends to shoot B but accidentally kills C, is he culpable?"

"Yes."

"You'll be fine."

"I could've answered that one," Raina says.

"Always thought you'd be good," I say.

"Hi," Raina says to Jessie.

"Oh, hi, Mrs. Claughlin."

"Stoltz. Ms. Stoltz," Raina says. "But, please, call me Raina."

Jessie blushes. "Sorry. Raina, of course."

Jessie offers her glass to the bartender for a refill. Raina asks for what she's having. I, at long last, get my whiskey. I distribute our drinks and the three of us slink off to the corner next to the stairwell.

"So, where exactly are you from?" Raina asks Jessie.

"My hometown is Wisner, Nebraska. We're known as the livestock capital of the state." Jessie laughs.

"Did you grow up on a farm?"

"Yeah, my family has swine and cattle. My dad's one of the proud holdouts, still maintaining a sizeable piece of his own father's land."

"Heavily subsidized, of course," I chime in between sips of Jameson.

"So do you know how to farm?" Raina asks.

"No," Jessie says. "I watched as a kid, but I didn't pay much attention, not seriously anyway. There was never any question that I'd pursue something else. Most young people leave these days. My dad likes to say, 'More and more corn, less and less people under sixty.'"

"If he wanted the family farm continued he shouldn't have had four girls," I say.

"True," Jessie says.

"Wow, four girls?" Raina says.

Jessie nods.

"So how was it being back?" I ask.

"It was wonderful. I did a lot of studying, of course. But I also got to spend a lot of time with my mom and my youngest sister. I also got my old bike out of the garage. Got a lot of good riding done. Those long, flat roads out there are so right for it."

"That's great," Raina says. "Tom never told me you were a cyclist. I'm thinking about buying a bike."

I nearly choke. "Do you even know how to ride a bike?" I say.

They both roll their eyes. "Raina," Jessie says, angling her shoulder in my wife's direction, "I'd be happy to go bike shopping with you. Help you make the right decision for your riding needs."

"Really?" Raina says.

"Yeah, we could go for rides together. It'll be fun."

They're getting along. Thank god for my incompetence. The photos from the park had come back blank. Every single one of them. Raina said I'd set the shutter speed too slow. Blurry gray: the color of the endearingly inept, rather than the traitorously adulterous.

"I'd love that," Raina says.

"To good rides!" I declare, each of us beaming as we raise our glasses.

* * *

SECOND FLOOR. I'M MAKING my rounds with the rest of the union heads. I'm on fire.

Amid a trickle of my steadily emerging associates is jovial John McDougall with two of his associates from the Federation of Allied Health Employees.

"There's the guy," McDougall says, nodding in my direction, "The man of the hour. Shaking hands and kissing babies, I see."

I chuckle and clink glasses with him. "You know me," I say.

"A well-deserved victory lap. You remember Drew Clark and Greg Donahue."

"Gentlemen," I say, shaking each of their hands. "It's good to see you, John."

"Tom Claughlin is the best ally you'll ever make in this business," McDougall continues, "but you'll hear more about that later."

"I'm afraid you'll have no choice," I say.

"I suppose you're right," McDougall says. "You seem well, Tom. Is your better half around?"

"Thanks, John. I feel well," I say. "Raina's around here somewhere. How are you? What's the word around the union these days? That was quite a victory we had for your receptionist."

"Yes, that's right." McDougall pauses. He glances at each of the other two men. "Everyone was very pleased with the result, Tom. But let's not talk about work at the party. We're here to enjoy ourselves, right?"

"Come on, John," I say. "You of all people should know guys like us can't separate our lives from our work. What would we have to talk about?" I gesture to Drew and Greg. They both smile politely. "Am I wrong? I was curious if you'd heard from Ms. Grant."

"From Ms. Grant?"

"Yes, from Doreen. How's she doing? I just thought—well, you know her. She's quite an expressive person. I just wondered if she'd been in touch. Ms. Engel and I grew quite fond of her." The three reps exchange looks. They seem nervous.

"Gentlemen," John says to his associates. "Will you excuse us?"

John and I make our way slowly through the crowd. The room's centerpiece is an antique carousel: wild-eyed wooden horses gripping polished metal in their teeth, frozen mid-stride.

"So, what's up?" I say, "That was a great deal we got her. I figured she would've been thrilled."

"Actually, Tom..." John's eyes drift downward toward his drink.

"What? Did something go wrong with the payment?"

"No, it's not that. The money came through on time and everything," John says, his stride slowing to a stop. "I've been meaning to tell you, Tom. I got a call last week. Ms. Grant never showed up to the clinic again."

"So, she decided not to take the job after all? Smart. I wouldn't have put myself back in that environment either."

"Look, I was hoping this could wait until after the party, it being your night and all."

"What? What happened?" I say.

"Tom, Ms. Grant passed away."

"She what?"

"It was a suicide."

"What?"

The lights in the room suddenly dim. There's a chime from the speakers, then a voice: "Your attention please. Everyone please make your way to the lobby. The toast will be taking place momentarily."

"Look, it's no one's fault. It seems Ms. Grant was a very troubled person. No one at the union knew her very well." McDougall puts his hand on my shoulder. "I'm sorry to have to break the news, Tom. It's a very sad thing."

The chime sounds again.

"Look, we'll talk more about this later. This is your night. Try not to think about it, okay?"

* * *

I'M HOLDING A PICKET sign amid a crowd of protesting tenants on Avenue C. The picture dissolves and a new one emerges of me in another crowd in front of the Capitol building. I have a mustache. I'm a young man. Then I'm shaking the mayor's hand on 125th and Lex. Ed Koch. Next I'm standing on the steps of the courthouse holding my law degree. I'm posing at a gathering with Cunningham and Levan. That was before they took on Klein. Then I'm speaking in a courthouse—I can't tell which. My mustache is gone.

Cunningham is delivering my toast from a small podium. A succession of laudatory quotes. I recognize names, though I can't follow what's being said. His tone is cheerful. I take another sip from my drink but the glass is empty.

Then the stock becomes grainy and starts to move. My wife is lifting my son from his crib. I remember this. Cal shot this scene of domestic bliss on 16 mm. The crowd erupts in sighs. On screen, Raina passes me the baby.

3

A dry, bitter taste. Cold and heavy. Gray. It's the sidewalk. And red. A brick wall. I'm on the ground.

"Best watch out." A voice. A man in a navy winter jacket. He steps over me and continues briskly down the street. "White man lying in the middle of the sidewalk..."

A sound. Scraping. Another man coming from the other direction. He's in bad shape, stooped, weathered.

"Rough night?" he asks. He inches forward a shopping cart, scraping the sidewalk with every lurch.

I sit up and draw my legs to my chest. He stops right in front of me.

"Gimme a dollar," he says.

His face is a network of wrinkles. His front teeth are missing save three yellow mounds, all to one corner. He's holding out his palm.

"C'mon," he says. "Fork it over, I know you got it." I'm still wearing my suit. "I need to eat breakfast too, don't I?"

I reach into my breast pocket. A flask-sized bottle. I must've picked it up last night. I try the other pocket and pull out my wallet. "Here," I say, handing him a few singles.

He stuffs the bills into his coat and resumes his jerky progression down the sidewalk.

I level my back against the wall and push myself up to my feet. The street sways like a schooner on open sea.

"Wait," I call, securing myself with one hand on the wall, "where am I?"

"Look up," the old man shouts in his gravelly rasp.

A placid, pale blue sky. A glowing plastic sign. McDonald's. There's an above-ground subway station: Coney Island. I must've fallen asleep on the train.

* * *

A DIRTY SCAB ON my cheek probably from the sidewalk. A day's worth of growth, eyes swollen and dark around the corners. My cell phone still won't turn on. Raina must be worried. Or mad. When did I leave the party? A splash of cold, crisp water. The last gulp of Jack Daniel's. Okay. Let's get you home.

I exit the bathroom and order a cup of McCafé. It's even worse than Dunkin' Donuts.

Today's Christmas Eve. I told Ben I'd take him to the Central Park Zoo to see the polar bears. Raina wanted the apartment to herself to finish some errands and prepare dinner. Plus, Ben loved them when I took him last year. He was two then. But this year he didn't even remember we'd gone. I think this time he'll remember. He's getting so smart.

Outside McDonald's. Stillwell and Mermaid Ave. Mermaid Ave. That's where Doreen worked. I'd love to just see the place. But I should really be getting back. What was the address again? The road only goes in one direction. It can't be far. Ben, my love, I'll be with you soon.

I start down Mermaid. Coney Island Bagels. Liberty Tax Center. Golden Krust. Our Lady of Solace Church where there's a nativity scene with Christ in a manger, wise men, Joseph, and Mary.

There it is, across from the church: the Coney Island Health Clinic. It's so small. I can't believe how bad she wanted to keep showing up to this place.

The door opens. It's a woman. She's got red scrubs on under her long, puffy down coat.

She crosses the street and walks right past me down Mermaid. She must be Doreen's replacement. I wonder how long ago she started. It couldn't have been long. Maybe she's still training. She turns, a block down, onto 16th Street, disappearing around the corner.

I jog down the block in her direction, stopping at the corner of 16th. She's on her cell phone, crossing the road diagonally. She probably lives on this street. I fall into step a few doors behind, on the opposite side of the street from her.

I'll just see where she's going. I can still get back before noon.

The woman reaches Neptune. It's a busier street. She's glancing back and forth waiting for the opportunity to cross. Shit. She just looked at me. Act natural. You're just going up 16th Street to meet a friend. Why not?

I stop at the corner of Neptune, too. Just avoid eye contact.

She starts walking. I better cross, too.

How am I going to get out of this?

There's a liquor store in the middle of the block. Wait. No more drinking today. I need to get back to the city.

I walk further up 16th. Her pace quickens. She's onto me. Damn.

Finally, she makes a right into a front yard. Plastic reindeer, vinyl siding, a porch with a screen door. She lets herself in. I stop and sigh. That was close.

I turn. Alright, back to Union Square.

"Hey!" Another voice. It's a muscular guy with a crew cut, jeans, and a Mets t-shirt. "What the hell do you think you're doing?"

I hurry down the sidewalk. A firm hand on my shoulder.

"Were you just following my wife?"

I turn to meet his stare. "No, no, I'm just looking for someone." He jerks my jacket, pulling me within inches of his face.

"Goddamn drunk. I don't want to see you on this block again, you got it? Get lost."

"Alright, I'm leaving, okay?" His grip loosens and he lets me go. I turn away. As I fix my suit collar I hear myself mutter, "Fucking asshole."

A sudden warmth, wet and running down the side of my face. He spat on me.

"Are you serious?" I say, swiveling to meet his eyes again. He's got his fists up in a fighting stance. "Are you fucking serious?!" Then I'm taking a swing at him, but he leans back and my fist just kisses the air.

His knuckles lodge into my gut. I can't breathe. I look up at my opponent, hoping for mercy. But he's already leaning in with another fist to my face.

* * *

LIMPING DOWN NEPTUNE. I'M bleeding. My head is pounding. There's a life-sized statue of a pirate. Captain Morgan. It's the liquor store. Aisles of bright, fluorescent-lit linoleum. I lean against the glass and stumble in.

4

I reach the top of the stairs at Union Square. Couples and families stroll past faceless street-dwellers. A glaring red ticker on a newsstand reads:

```
... 33°F ... 11:49 DECEMBER 25 2005
    ... MERRY CHRISTMAS ...
```

Jesus. Where have I been?

There's a paper stuck in the slush on the sidewalk. *The Daily News*. It's already a few days old. In big white letters the cover reads: "Nobody Wins." There's a photo of an M15 bus. "In this strike everyone has lost: the workers, the union, the MTA, New York business and most of all, you."

Raina will be on the couch reading to Ben. Or maybe Ben will be reading to her. He's committed *Yertle the Turtle* to memory. He'll drop the book when he sees me and come running.

"It's Christmas," he'll say.

"I'm not too late, am I?"

"No, Daddy, you're not too late."

Raina will hold back, arms folded, skeptical about my absence. I'll walk over to her. I'll kiss her on the forehead, apologize about my appearance. I'll tell her not to worry about my black eye. I'm alright. I'll take a shower, change into fresh clothes. I'll make lunch for everyone. Later, we'll go for a walk. Get hot chocolate. Maybe we'll go to the movies.

But my apartment is empty. At the doorway to the bedroom, I listen for breathing. It's silent. Both beds are empty. Elmo is gone, too. The tree is there but all the presents are missing. They must've done Christmas somewhere else.

I start the shower.

Raina sits across from me in the tub, an open champagne bottle between her legs. The radio is tuned to a station that seems to play only Edith Piaf. It's our honeymoon. She takes a swig and passes me the bottle. Her fingers are like prunes.

"I'm starving," she says. We've been in here for hours, giggling and making love.

"Ready to brave the cold?" I say. We were so in love. The only couple naive enough to think a wintertime honeymoon in Montreal would be a good idea.

I cut the shower and reach for a towel.

Seventeen new messages. I dress and put my jacket and hat back on. There's a bottle cap in my jacket pocket. Jim Beam.

Outside the apartment, the sky has darkened. My stomach clenches again. What restaurants are open on Christmas morning? It's so quiet. Snow is beginning to fall. I look up and down 17th Street in each direction.

Then I see her. Raina. She's with someone. He's got Ben in his arms. Is that Frank? They're at the corner, waiting for the light to change. She brushes a lock of hair from her face. A bus passes on Park Avenue South. Our eyes meet. She steps off the curb. The light turns white.

Acknowledgments

I'm so appreciative of Lisa Weinert for seeing the potential in my book and of Tyson Cornell, Alice Marsh-Elmer, and Julia Callahan for bringing it to print. I'd also like to thank Deborah Brown for being an early supporter, along with Jules de Balincourt. I'm indebted to Sam Tillman, Nicole Ball, Adam Brown, Paige Newman, Jason Krugman, Jen Krieger, Alex Feld, Nils Aspengren, and Krista Knight, who came to my apartment and sat while I read early drafts to them. Jesse McDonough and Elana Adler were wonderful roommates who allowed me solitude while I wrote this. Lydia Bell provided love and support. Thank you to Patrick Kattner, Rebekah Potter, Lindsay Benedict, Rhice Manelli Brewer, Logan Kruger and Dawn Skorczewski for being early, insightful readers. Adam Wilson told me at the age of thirteen what music to listen to and what books to read, and he continues to introduce me to new, *inspiring authors of which he's one. Christi Hansen opened widely my way of thinking; I didn't have anything I needed to write about before I met her. Chris Spain, Pat C. Hoy II, and Howard Norman imparted their wisdom to me; their teachings resonate. Courtney Foster kept me honest and happy. Ben Lehn designed an elegant cover. Angie Hughes stepped in with last minute copyediting. The Bushwick community—in particular Anna D'Agrosa and Scott McGibney and the baristas at the Wyckoff Starr and the bartenders at Pearl's, Tandem, and The Northeast Kingdom, especially Sam Coffey—makes it hard to want to live anywhere else. It would be difficult to overstate my gratitude to Roarke Menzies for his guidance and vision in the editorial process and for the friendship we share. I'm excited for all the work we're going to create together. And thank you to my family: Mom, Dad, and Emily.*